Death Dreamer

Melanie Miller Hollis

This book is dedicated to every person who has been abused…to those who have been open about it and to those who have chosen to keep their harrowing experience secretly hidden…whatever you are going through, or whatever you have been through, know that abuse does not define you. You have value. You are strong. I've been there. And I see you.

This book is also dedicated to every person who has battled depression of any kind. I've battled depression as well and understand what a lonely, tiring journey it can be. Be strong and take courage; it will pass. Hang on to what you know to be true. God is real. He understands. Nothing takes Him by surprise. And He truly is as close as the shade on your right hand.

Finally, to each of you who take the time to read my books, to message me, and to give me positive feedback….thank you! I have words in my heart that need to be written, so I write.

ISBN: 0692751432

ISBN 13: 9780692751435

4

Chapter 1

Fog hugged the town tightly that morning, forcing an aroma from the nearby paper mill that could be likened to rotten eggs to permeate every square inch, or so it seemed to Wills. Still partially hungover from a three-day party binge that had left him in a stupor, the young college student sat slumped on a monstrous brown leather sofa in a coffee shop near Cleveland, Tennessee's Lee University campus, hoping the smell of fresh brew would cover the stench. He couldn't recall the last time he'd taken a real shower with shampoo and body wash. His hair was disheveled and his shirt untucked, and he wore Windsor plaid pajama pants that tied loosely around his waist, draping over flip-flops he'd owned since the tenth grade. He remembered this because he'd gotten them just prior to his family's spring-break trip to the Florida coast that year. It was the last time they had vacationed at the beach together.

Sniffing his armpits to see how badly he smelled, Wills chuckled, considering that he might be the source of the sickening smell instead of the old paper mill. Around him, students made love to their favorite coffee combinations without a care in the world. That used to be him.

Two years after his engagement to a former cult leader's daughter, life had gone from plain vanilla ice cream to rocky road. Somewhere along the way he had gotten lost; not even a small sliver of his former self was intact. His parents' divorce had shaken him, but the fact that his mom was not much like a mom anymore was almost too much for him to bear. Mary had joined a gym, had treated herself to a makeover, and had even gone out on a couple of dates. Most of her prospects came from an online dating service, which blew his mind. He had (not so politely) refused to meet any of her prospects and would never get used to his mother asking for dating advice.

Crushing a now-empty paper cup with both hands, Wills brought his arm back and threw it like a football into the recycling bin while whispering aloud, "Touchdown." Why couldn't his own life be recycled? Reformed and renewed into something better, or at least into something that resembled normal? As he lumbered out of the coffee shop and down the sidewalk toward the two-story white house on Ocoee Street, he dreaded facing his grandparents most of all. GiGi and Poppy had purchased the house from his parents after they had nearly lost it due to financial woes. They couldn't bear to let Mary, Tate, Miss Charity, and him lose their home; after all, this was the only home the kids had ever known. Mary, especially, appreciated the sacrificial gesture. Recently, however, there had been some not-so-minor changes. The retirees, in a whirlwind decision, had sold their own home to move into the Ocoee Street house. Mary, of course, thought it a grand idea since she would now have live-in babysitters who would be right under her nose at all times. Taking care of a child who has Down syndrome is a twenty-four- hour-a-day job that becomes much more manageable with teamwork. Wills understood that all too well. Their moving in, however, lessened the chances of his parents ever reconciling. The college-aged, former quarterback and golden boy was losing hope.

As he caught sight of the house, Wills allowed his mind to turn to his sister, Tate. Still homeschooled, a young teen caught between being a girl and womanhood, she was perhaps the most responsible, levelheaded member of the entire family. It baffled Wills to consider how she had gone through all the same drama-laced junk he'd gone through, and yet she remained steadfast in all things, especially in her faith. She may have been younger, but he admired her strength. A beautiful teenage girl who had boys chasing after her relentlessly, she held true to her decision to wait for the right one to come along. And that was just fine with Wills. Climbing up the front steps, he caught a reflection of himself in the glass storm door, which served to protect the massive mahogany front door. He quickly ran down a long list of faces in his mind: faces that belonged to girls he had carelessly used and tossed aside. Purity was definitely a thing of his past, as was God.

Wills slowly pressed the latch on the front door handle and pushed to open the door without making much of a sound. Slipping inside, he gently closed both doors in the same fashion. It was early, so he knew his mother, grandparents, and his aunt Viv would be gathered around the kitchen table drinking coffee and cackling like a gaggle of geese. He was right. His aunt, recently married, was preparing to take in a couple of foster kids until her own womb was in full bloom. Filled with so much spiritual pride regarding the subject, her cackle was the loudest of all. It rang through the house. The woman was all about it, feeling high and mighty, haughty, and self-righteous. Wills immediately heard her bragging about how she and her husband were praying for God to lead them in this new parenting endeavor, but Wills wasn't fooled, and so he assumed God wasn't fooled either. His aunt had always been more about show than anything else.

He made his way down the back hall and peeked into Miss Charity's room. There they were, exactly as he knew he would find them. The Little Miss was tucked beneath Tate's arm, both propped up by a heap of fluffy pillows, and they were watching reruns featuring Grover, Big Bird, Elmo, and Cookie Monster. A crown, with most of its rhinestones missing, graced the head of the youngest Montgomery, Miss Charity. To him, she was indeed the princess of all princesses.

Without saying a word, Wills entered the room to join them. Miss Charity, who had been madly in love with her big brother since the day she was born, left the comfort of Tate and climbed upon his lap, giggling. He took her crown and placed it upon his own head, and she responded by snatching it right back. Tate teasingly punched his arm just before laying her head on his shoulder. They were together, safe from the world, in the comfort of that little room until GiGi came bursting in, jerking them back into the wiles of their crazy existence.

"Wills Montgomery!" she hollered. "How long have you been in here while we've been out there waiting for you?"

GiGi stood with her hands firmly on her hips. Wills caught her blazing stare for only a moment and then turned to look around the room, not out of disrespect, but because he felt lost and ashamed.

After getting no reply from her grandson, GiGi continued. "Young man, I'm going to go back out there and inform your momma that you've been back here monkeying around while you were supposed to be meeting with us. And if you don't get to that kitchen table real quick, I will return in just a few minutes to jerk a knot in your tail." She huffed and stomped one foot and, with obvious outrage, exited the room. Drama was his grandmother's strongest suit.

Wills didn't say a word for a few minutes; instead, he continued to look around his little sister's room, taking in all the details that made it perfect for her. The walls had been painted many different colors over the years. As Mary's moods changed, her little girl's room seemed to follow and reflect those ups and downs. For the time being, three of the walls were covered in pale lavender, with a fourth wall painted with a deep purple chalkboard paint. Thoughtfully noting all the drawings left on that wall by the hand of the chalk artist who was still seated in his lap, he wished she could speak words and tell him what each mark was intended to be. Where did her imagination take her? What were her dreams? Was one of the drawings of her and him? He couldn't tell. Down syndrome has a way of making muscle coordination and manipulation difficult, so her artwork looked erratic and unintentional, though he knew it was far more than that to Miss Charity.

"Little princess," he said, carefully moving the scrumptious bundle that was Miss Charity back under Tate's arm before rolling off the bed, "you have drawn some beautiful pictures." Catching the eyes of the two girls he loved more than the air he took in to breathe, Wills gasped at their beauty and grinned. "You know what?" he asked. "I think your big brother needs to draw you a very special picture, and it will probably be your most favorite picture of all, Miss Charity."

He took a piece of chalk and drew two stick figures holding hands, one much taller than the other and the smaller one donning a big bow. He then placed a heart between them. "That is you and big brother," he said, looking pleased with himself.

Clumsily shuffling his feet a couple of steps to his right in order to draw Tate's eye, he drew another stick figure with two curly strands protruding from a big smiling

14

face, depicting long hair belonging to a happy girl. Pointing to this new stick figure, which was standing off by herself, away from the other two stick figures who were holding hands, Wills continued. "And that is Tater Bug, who loves you lots, but not nearly as much as I love you."

Tate, in response, picked up a pillow and hurled it at him. Within seconds, he pounced back on the bed and tickled his sisters until they were breathless with giggles. Miss Charity, elated, wrapped her arms around the necks of her big brother and big sister, simultaneously pulling them in close to her. "Princess, we love you," Wills whispered softly as a tear escaped from his eye and rolled down his cheek. He wiped it away, unhooked her arm from his neck, and quickly darted out to face the firing squad.

Chapter 2

Philip, who had never loved any other woman but Mary, could not adapt to the life of a bachelor. He'd created a makeshift apartment for himself in the building that housed his business and had worked every hour he wasn't asleep to rebuild all he had lost after news of the scam he had unwittingly been involved in, as well as his affair with Bonnie Cutless, had taken its cruel toll. More than once he'd considered ending his life. Thoughts of driving off a bridge, taking a bottle of scripts, or hooking up a hose to the tailpipe of his car while it was parked inside a garage had plagued him. *Dared* him. Having lost more than twenty pounds, the Chief was now a mere shell of his former self, sorely ashamed of all his life had become.

It was a Saturday morning, and he had showered and was waiting for his one remaining friend to come by for their weekly visit. Carrying a nondescript white bag filled with sausage, gravy, and biscuits from the Rebel restaurant, Preacher Walker arrived right on time as expected. The two sat around a small table, prayed a prayer of thanks, and began to dig in.

"So how has your week been, Philip?" the pastor asked with a smile, already knowing what the response would be. The older man could nearly recite what the once proud husband, father, and businessman would say. He'd begin by recounting all his regrets, continue by explaining why he deserved all the heartache he was experiencing, and then end by questioning whether his life would ever be worth living again. The pastor would listen because he understood Philip's deep need to talk things through, but his response was always the same as well: "Mary, Wills, and Tate may be able to learn to move on and live their lives without you, but not Miss Charity. Her world is so small, Philip. Just remember, that little doll needs you, and I reckon she always will."

Philip assumed Preacher Walker came each week for the sake of friendship, but it was more than that. Each Saturday morning early on, an unseen angel would wake the white-haired saint with thoughts of Philip, needling him until he had no choice but to get out of bed and pay a visit. That angel knew how Philip was hanging on by a mere thread; he also knew how much Philip counted on those meetings. Sorrow is a funny thing that can surely fool you. A man can walk around looking like he's got life pretty well under control, while all the while he's drowning. That summed up Philip Montgomery to a tee.

After the pastor left, Philip hurried to take a shower. He had received a phone call from a potential investor during the week who was sending his assistant to look at one of Philip's available commercial properties. At ten-thousand square feet, a one-year lease of that property would put him back in the black. He was prepared to pour on his sales skills like never before as he allowed himself to dream of buying that old Ocoee house back from his former in-laws. He kept in touch with GiGi and

Poppy on a regular basis, unbeknownst to anyone else in the family, and they wished for the same thing. They were *for* Philip, not against him. Leasing this property would be a first step, a big step, in making that dream a reality.

Philip was too busy trying to find the keys to the property, pulling off local statistical information from the Internet, and sprucing up his office to notice when the black Lexus pulled into the parking lot. It wasn't until Bonnie Cutless waltzed into his office that he had a clue it was almost time for the meeting to begin.

"What's up, Chief...oh, I mean Philip?" She giggled. "I nearly lost my manners for a moment and completely forgot that it is only 'Mary, Mary, Quite Contrary' who can call you Chief." Sarcasm dripped from every word.

He jerked his neck around fast, turning so fiercely that the movement caused a shooting pain to run clear up from his shoulder blade to the top of his head. Grabbing his neck, he moaned and flopped down into his desk

19

chair with a thud. "Bonnie?" was all the poor guy could manage.

Gliding over to his desk, she put both her hands on his desk and leaned over, placing her breasts, which were cupped tightly by a pushup bra beneath a tight black jersey dress, in clear view. "So, you do remember me? It's been way too long, sugar, don't you think?"

Philip's mind was in a whirl, and his neck was throbbing. "Good Lord, my stupid neck is killing me," he managed, still careful to keep his eyes averted from Bonnie. Undeterred, she stayed her ground, waiting for the moment when he would look up and get a load of her. This was a day she had been carefully calculating for some time, and not one moment would go to waste.

"Want me to give you a deep tissue massage for that neck problem?" she offered. "Massages are my thing... but I'm sure you remember that, don't you, Philip?"

"No, no, no…no need for that," he stammered. "The pain is easing."

A mental picture of Preacher Walker returning to his office and finding Bonnie rubbing his neck caused Philip's heart to nearly beat its way up to his throat. Taking a deep breath, he finally allowed himself to look at the blonde bombshell who was at the top of his list of regrets.

Boobs…of course, boobs, he thought to himself before forcing his eyes to meet hers. She noticed.

"Like what you see?" she asked flirtatiously, batting her eyes.

Determined not to encourage her, Philip asked, "What are you doing here?" As the words slipped from his mouth, he wondered whether she could hear his voice shaking.

Instead of responding, Bonnie found a chair, pulled it over, and centered it right in front of Philip's desk. As she sat down, Philip wondered if she would flash him like she had done in the past. Bonnie Cutless had never been one to wear panties. His groin tingled, and in that moment he hated that he was a man.

"Ummm, Bonnie," he said, his voice still wavering and his mouth now quivering, "I'm expecting a client to show up any minute, so now is not a good time for us to talk. I'm sorry."

Bonnie laughed, not missing a beat. "I am your client."

Her legs were crossed; spiked heels with laces that crisscrossed all the way up her calves caught his attention. She knew he would like them. Philip had a thing for shoes.

He brought his eyes back up to meet hers. "You're my client?" he asked, clearly confused. "What are you talking about, Bonnie?"

It took only a few minutes for Bonnie to explain that she had picked up a job and that her new employer invested primarily in commercial real estate. However, within seconds, Philip realized this "new job" was more of an opportunity for *her* to invest in *him*.

Chapter 3

The family meeting with Wills didn't go well. His drinking and partying was out of control, so something drastic had to be done. When Mary, GiGi, and Poppy explained to Wills that he was going to have to move out and find a place of his own, that they could no longer support his behavior by allowing him to live in their home, he had been caught off guard. The beloved firstborn was expecting to be yelled at, but kicked out of his home?

When Wills stormed out of the house with a laundry sack full of clothes, slamming the door behind him, Viv was the first to speak up, assuring everyone that they had made the best choice, the *only* choice, in giving the rebellious young man a needed wake-up call. Mary wasn't so sure. If this was the *best* choice, the *only* choice, then why did she feel as though she'd been punched in the gut?

"You know this is on you, don't you, Mary?" GiGi's words were curt and pointed. "That freak cult show you got caught up in has screwed your son up royally."

At the mention of her involvement with the Lost Tribe Fellowship, Mary bristled. She'd been vulnerable after learning of Philip's brief affair with Bonnie Cutless, and when Miss Charity began having complications with her heart again, Mary fell prey to the cult's promises of God's healing. They saw her as weak, so they had pounced, filling her mind with what seemed to be scriptural truth, but what ended up being a masterful manipulation of God's word. Philip and Mary had money; that's all the cult leaders cared about. Now, their marriage was over, their money was gone, and the rest of the family was a mess.

Poppy knew his wife's words were like a dagger, cutting Mary to the bone at a time when she needed support, so he interjected, "Now wait just a doggone minute, woman." (He only referred to his wife as "woman" when he was extremely ticked off.) He continued. "This ain't Mary's fault or anyone else's, for that matter, so pipe it down!" The man was no dummy and knew he'd pay a hefty price for standing up to his wife once they were alone, but he didn't back down. "We've all given Wills chance after chance after chance to get his act together, but he refuses. At some point, enough is enough. He's an adult now, making very bad, and sometimes dangerous, adult choices. It's our job to let him see that we love him too much to accept the choices he's making right now."

"Pops is right…this isn't anyone's fault," Viv said, agreeing with her father. "Listen, we have to stick together as a united front. Now is not the time to turn on one another. Not to mention, Mom, that Sam and I are still a part of that freak cult show, so I'd appreciate it if you'd be a little nicer when speaking about our religion."

"Religion…is that what you're calling it?" GiGi's face was blood red, and her eyes bugged out that they nearly rolled out of their sockets. Even so, for the marriage union of Sam and Viv, she was ready to take full blame. "Listen, Viv, we are all fully aware that you are still part of the freak cult show because you are wearing the cult skirts clear to your ankle bones and donning that stupid lace doily on your head. Curse my devilish plan to save Mary from the cult by dragging you into it as an imposter…honestly, I thought you'd have more sense than to drink the Kool-Aid and fall for one of them fuzzy faced bearded men, but no…my kids have all gone to heck in a hand basket." Standing up from the table, she grabbed her coffee cup and marched over to the sink to wash it out.

Viv, not happy with her mother's attack, fired back. "I'll remind you, Mother, that *my* life, compared to Mary's, is very normal…happy and normal." Then turning to Mary, she added, "No offense to you, Mare Bear, but your life truly is a train wreck."

GiGi couldn't take it anymore. The scuff with Wills had pushed her too far. Instinctively, she turned the sink's water nozzle toward Viv, who was still seated at the table. When the cold water hit the back of Viv's head, she shot straight up and let out a shrill scream. GiGi was not deterred. "Your life is happy and normal? Normal my eye!" she yelled, still spraying the water. "Wake up, dagnabbit! You are in a cult!"

It seemed all the females were destined to turn on one another. GiGi blamed Mary for Wills's drinking habit, Mary resented her mother for placing all the blame on her, and Viv hated that *her* family was not the center of attention, especially since she was a newlywed and was soon to become a first-time mom through the foster care system. Poppy once again jumped in and came to the rescue, grabbing the spray nozzle from GiGi's hands and getting sprayed himself in the process.

"What in God's name is wrong with all of you?" he chuckled, noting how Viv's long hair was soaking wet and her hair doily was now barely hanging on. Mary ran to get her sister a towel while Poppy continued. "Surely to God we've all got better sense than to turn on one another during a time when we need to band together like thieves."

"I, for one, am trying to band together, Pops," GiGi replied, chiming in as if she were a victim of an unfair circumstance. "You know I am a peacemaker at heart…I have been since birth…just like the good Lord Himself. It's my gifting."

Viv took a deep breath, ready to aim some fiery words right back at her mother, but Poppy quickly gave her a harsh shake of his head.

"You got something to say, Viv?" GiGi spoke up, slathering sass like butter on a biscuit.

Again Poppy shook his head in his daughter's direction, so Viv, going against every instinct within her, backed down. She was furious about being sprayed by the water and felt as though she had been unfairly attacked, but opting not to fan her momma's flames any further for her

29

dad's sake, she decided to change the subject. "So, on the subject of the two little girls Sam and I will be fostering, how do you all feel about giving them a party? You know, to celebrate them moving in with us?"

"God, that's all we need during a time like this…two little foster kids who are going to turn our lives even more upside down," GiGi raged, feeling full of herself. "But that's just like you, Viv, to make everything about you." Grabbing her jacket, the spitfire stormed toward the front door in a huff. "I hope y'all will excuse me while I go take a walk and try to cool down before I have a full-on heart attack…my pulse is racing!" And just like that, she was out the door, leaving the house calm and peaceful.

"She is a nightmare," Viv complained, still irritated by her mother's ill temper.

Mary, walking in with a towel, threw it in her sister's direction and spoke frankly. "It takes one to know one, sis."

Poppy, in turn, giggled. It was the truth. The two were clones of each other.

The family was hung. They would have to give Viv's foster children a party, even though the timing couldn't be worse. Although Poppy and GiGi had begged Viv and Sam to wait awhile and enjoy some time being married to one another before starting a family, the two had been married for nearly six months, which, according to the Lost Tribe Fellowship congregation, was long enough. By the standards of their pseudo-faith, a bun should've already been baking in Viv's oven. Needless to say, Viv and Sam were feeling the pressure. They had been working at making a baby the "natural" way but so far hadn't had any luck. According to the elders of their church, infertility was a sign that they needed to explore adoption. Viv had been reluctant at first, given that in her experience working with the school system she had seen many foster children who carried tremendous loads of baggage, but Sam had insisted.

31

Viv remembered the first time Sam lost his temper with her. They had been married for two weeks, and it was over something so trivial. She had laundered some of his clothes and hung them in his closet. She couldn't recall whether she had been in a rush that day or not, but when he came home from work that night and opened his closet, he had screamed for her to meet him in the bedroom. When she entered, he'd thrown armfuls of clothes (still attached to hangers) at her. Having never seen this side of Sam, she was shocked and just stood there as the clothes hit her face and her chest. It didn't physically hurt, of course, but it was demeaning…and his words that day still stuck with her: *"I'm glad to know that I married an idiot. It is no wonder no man ever wanted you before. You can't even do a simple load of laundry, which a monkey could be taught to do."*

She had tried to interrupt him, but any attempt was met with even louder, harsher words.

"Shut up, you mutt! I take care of my clothes because I work hard for the money I earn…look how you've hung my things up without any thought or care to what belongs to me. Everything I own will be a wrinkled mess. But let's take a look at your closet…"

He'd then dragged her by the arm to her closet, where he proceeded to dump all her clothes onto the floor. He then unzipped his pants and urinated on them before stomping out of the room and leaving the house.

Viv, in response, had sat on her bed and bawled. She didn't know what else to do. Always fiery, on that day, in that moment, she felt more like a whipped puppy. She was married to this man. *Married.* Life as Viv knew it had forever changed.

Chapter 4

Philip's parents had moved away from Cleveland just after Tate was born. This was due to a corporate transfer to Florida, which included a hefty pay raise and a promotion for his father, but they had hated to leave their grandchildren and had only managed to see them a handful of times each year since. Recently retired, Philip's father was excited to call his son to give him the good news. They were moving back within the month.

The two were somewhat aware of the issues their son was dealing with, but he had painted it all with as tame a brush as possible. The divorce, he had told them, was because Mary was battling depression over Miss Charity's heart scare, along with the fact that Wills was growing up too fast and had left for college. That was actually all he had told them, which meant the news of their return had left him as nervous as a long-tailed cat in a room full of rocking chairs. They had assured him they would be helping him to put his marriage back together once they were settled. Poor fools. They didn't know the half of it.

Philip's foundation was shifting, and all he could do was to go with it. The news of his parents had taken him off guard, but so had Bonnie's arrival back on the scene. The day he'd spent with her had gone surprisingly well. It had started off with her acting like a tease, but as it turned out, as she described it, she had only been playing a game with him for laughs. He was relieved but also embarrassed that he'd thought her to still be interested in him. After signing the documents for the lease arrangement, the two had caught up at dinner. A small candlelit table awaited them at the locally owned Roma's Italian restaurant. It might have appeared romantic, but Bonnie had treated the occasion as purely business.

"I'm still married to Carter," she said with a sheepish grin, while pulling apart a piece of fresh Italian bread. "I don't think we'll ever officially divorce, even though, as you know, we haven't had a marriage in years. He's still a workaholic, so I barely lay eyes on him…and I can't remember to save my life when I last had a real conversation with the man." Bonnie confided in Philip as if he were the dearest friend she had. "Crew, of course, is traveling around to other countries, exploring the world and doing mission work. I guess I have Preacher Walker to thank for that."

Bonnie seemed lonely, and Philip could relate to her on that level. His own life had changed so much since the divorce. Accustomed to seeing his children every day, he now only saw them by appointment. The custody arrangement was upside down and awkward for him, but during his conversation with Bonnie, he never let on.

"After our affair," she continued, rattling on while eating her bread, "when I woke up and really saw all the damage I'd done to your family and to my own son, I left town and got help. Can you believe I checked myself into a long-term mental health facility?"

Philip was proud of her for seeking help and told her so. She teared up as she considered how kind this man was to her, even though she had once relentlessly seduced him.

"I met my boss's wife while I was there," she explained, still in awe of Philip's kindness toward her. "She was one of my therapists and believed a professional job, one that required responsibility, would offer the extra healing I needed."

Philip hung on her every word. The transformation was remarkable. Bonnie really did appear to be a different individual. She'd even explained that hearing about his recent troubles gave her the courage to try to right her wrongs with him. "Like I told you, my interest in you now is purely professional, Philip. I was playing with you earlier today by flashing my sexy bra…because you know how I love sexy lingerie…but, honestly, I have no ulterior motives here. I just want to try to make up for all the problems I've caused."

"The divorce was not your fault, Bonnie," Philip offered, hoping to put her mind at ease. "I have made many mistakes with Mary."

Bonnie, noticing the sorrow in Philip's eyes, quickly changed the subject. "Guess what the best part of therapy was for me?" she asked with a perky smile.

He was clueless but couldn't help but feel a bit drawn to the woman who was showing such interest in spending time with him. Did his heart skip a beat when she smiled?

"I no longer have my obsessive-compulsive disorder issues." She was clearly so proud of herself. "You have no idea how much OCD ruled my every waking minute, Philip. I used to count each stair I took and was hung up on how many times I brushed my hair. I washed my hands at least fifty times a day, and everything on my to-do list had to be accomplished on the hour, the quarter hour, or the half hour." She laughed out loud at herself thinking about it. "I was a bigger nutcase than you can imagine, and you were sleeping with me…most of the time on the half hour."

Bonnie belly laughed, and Philip joined in. Self-deprecating humor is an admirable quality, and it drew Philip in even more. With all the ice broken, the two enjoyed catching up on everything. Things he had held back from his many talks with Preacher Walker, he freely spilled to Bonnie. No judgment would befall Philip from her since she'd had the most whacked-out, crazy past of anyone he'd ever met. They discussed the irony of how Wills had turned away from God while Crew had made a commitment to devote his entire life to God and then debated the exciting pull of the cult versus the drudgery of the church's long-standing establishment. Philip opened up his heart to Bonnie Cutless. He cried and confessed all his mistakes, and she listened.

Chapter 5

The arrival of Sam and Viv's new foster daughters occurred the same week as the arrival of Philip's parents back into town. Philip, who was still very much involved in the lives of his children, was invited to the party. During the conversation with Viv, he had mentioned that his parents were returning to town, and surprisingly, his former sister-in-law had graciously invited them to come, too. Philip, believing Viv was simply being courteous, had been reluctant to accept the invitation. Viv, though, had pushed hard, urging him to attend. Consequently, because he longed to see Mary on any and every occasion possible, he had relented and agreed to show up, even if only for a little while.

Viv's purpose for inviting Philip and his parents was not purely innocent. A calculated move on her part, she hoped to begin this bout of motherhood and family on the best foot possible. In her mind, these girls presented an opportunity for a brand-new beginning with Sam. She hoped Philip's presence, along with his parents, would move her mother's attention far enough away from her and her little girls that it would lessen the chances of a blowup of any sort. Anyone who'd known GiGi for any time at all knew she was always the unpredictable firecracker in any group setting. And if the old bird was going to explode, Viv would much rather the fallout be left upon Philip and his parents. This was going to be a pivotal night for Viv, and she didn't want anything or anyone to ruin it. Sam had already demanded a celebratory event with no drama from her, and she needed to make sure Sam got what he wanted.

Viv, in her usual over-the-top style, had asked her sister if she could have carte blanche to decorate. Mary, who was not up for the celebration, had quickly obliged, and so the old Ocoee house had officially been transformed into a princess paradise, complete with twinkling lights dazzling all the trees in the front yard. Taking center stage in the great room, covered in hot pink lace, stood a grand table embellished with tall glass urns that were bursting with homemade pink gummy candy drops and fluffy marshmallows coated in pink sprinkles. Glass-footed platters topped with white-chocolate-covered cake pops also adorned the table, enhancing the grandeur of the regal theme. The highlight, though, was the Cinderella glass slipper that had been filled with bite-size princess-crown sugar cookies.

Silver metallic eyelash fabric hung from the ceiling, billowing in soft poufs and accenting the large pastel crepe-paper flowers that had been hung with simple fishing lines throughout the space. No detail had been forgotten; Viv had thought of everything. The two newest members of the gang would experience a perfect evening.

Ruby and Rose were four and six respectively. Biracial, and sharing the same birth parents, the two sported long corkscrew curls. Had it not been for a slight difference in height, the two sisters could have easily passed for twins.

Both were willowy thin, and if their larger-than-life hair was a constant wow factor, then their brown, puppy dog eyes were the show stealer. The girls were outwardly gorgeous in every way, but what was hidden inside them was not beautiful at all. Their short lives had been tumultuous. The girls' mom, a meth addict, had neglected and abused them. Their birth father was presumed dead. Their grandparents on both sides were uninterested and uninvolved. Sam and Viv would be the fifth foster parents for the two spunky sisters, who could hardly wait for their princess party.

"It's so nice to meet you girls," GiGi said, bending down on one knee to greet them both as soon as they entered. "I wanted to be the first one to give you each a gift, because I want to be your favorite person in the whole world." GiGi beamed as she handed them each a gift bag. "You're gonna love your GiGi!"

Ruby and Rose tore into the bags without hesitation to find tutus, princess crowns, pink lipstick, and glitter for their hair. "You can't really be a princess without some glam, can you?" The old bird giggled, watching the two shimmy into their tutus.

Sam gave GiGi a sideways glance that didn't go unnoticed. "Are you all right, Sam?" she asked.

"I just don't want to spoil them," he replied. "They haven't even walked into the house, and you're already loading them up with gifts."

"You're darned tootin' I'm gussying these girls up with gifts," she said, shooting the girls a silly wink. "And this is just the beginning. I'm gonna spoil these girls rotten!" She opened her arms wide, and the girls responded by giving her hugs. "That's right. There's not one thing wrong with glam."

Not wanting to Sam to have the chance to ruin her moment, GiGi shooed the two dolls off into the great room to find the rest of the family. Sam didn't move.

"What is your problem?" she asked him, climbing to her feet. "A gift bag full of goodies is good for those girls… Viv said neither one of them has ever had very much. This is a party, am I right, Sam I Am?"

Sam, who still wore his long ratty beard as a sign of his "faith" in God, had become more comfortable with vocalizing his opinions when it came to Viv's parents. And he despised it when GiGi referred to him as Sam I Am.

"We are in charge of those girls, GiGi…not you," he shot back, not hiding the fact that he was a bit hot around the collar. In the beginning, he had seemed shy and backward to GiGi and Poppy, but they had slowly but surely come to find him to be one who enjoyed speaking up…and even stirring things up. He continued. "I just want you to know right off that I am their daddy, and I will decide if and when gifts are appropriate before they are given from now on," he declared, fully expecting his remark to get a rise out of his mother-in-law.

"First off, 'Daddy,' you aren't their daddy," she corrected him with a sneer. "You are a foster daddy…and there is a difference. Second of all, this is a party at *my house,* and when I throw a party at *my house*, using *my money,* I will purchase whatever the heck I want to purchase. Got it?" GiGi was counting off each point with her fingers. Holding up her third finger, with her voice climbing to a full throaty pitch, she preached on. "And number three, Sam I Am…this is a free country, and you're not gonna censor any gift I give to anybody!"

Without giving Sam the opportunity to respond, GiGi clicked her wedges and was out of sight within seconds.

Sam, checking his temper, decided to let it go. He would have a talk with Viv about her mother's bawdiness when they got home, after the girls were in bed asleep. She would pay for her mother's sins. It was only fair—after all, someone needed to pay. He then paraphrased a Bible verse beneath his breath as he moseyed over to join the others: "Our God is a jealous God, so He visits the sins of the mothers upon their daughters for generations."

The party was a complete success by any measure. Ruby and Rose were charmers, bewitching all who were eager to greet them. Drawing from all the attention given to them, they entertained the guests by singing their favorite songs. Viv had thought ahead to set up a small wooden stage and had flanked it with curtains. The girls, high on sugar, had utilized it fully.

Philip and his parents did stop by, but they didn't stay very long. Having been raised in true Southern fashion, they each knew their proper place, and their proper place was actually anywhere but at the princess party. Miss Charity, happy to see her paternal grandparents and missing her brother Wills, had barely let them leave. She'd held onto their legs for dear life as they worked to pry her fingers away. Tate, too, was thrilled to see them. Philip noticed and decided it might actually be a positive thing for his parents to move back to Cleveland. They deserved the opportunity to open up their hearts and be real grandparents, the kind who are involved in all the day-to-day drudgery but who take time to relish every second of it for the sake of love. And so he would gladly give them that chance.

GiGi, hot around the collar and still in a whirl about her spat with Sam, didn't notice Philip or his parents. She was too busy using her adrenaline rush to graciously wait on the guests, taking care to serve them well. She made sure stomachs were filled and that all who would accept took a little something sweet home with them. Curious about her son-in-law and his kooky behavior, she took time to watch him closely. He seemed to dote on Viv and gave plenty of attention to his new foster daughters, and that pleased her. No matter her own misgivings, the woman was for family above all. If Viv was happy with the bearded cult man, then she would put up with his smart mouth.

As for Mary, she was amiable to all. A constant splattering of cheer illuminated her face, belying her true feelings. It was not easy seeing Philip in the old white house. It had been their home, the place they had refurbished with their own hands, that had welcomed each of their children, and where she used to feel the safest because of him. The Ocoee Street edifice, once a symbol of the strength of her marriage, now stood as a monument proclaiming their many failings. True love had failed.

***

After all the guests were long gone, Miss Charity's angel guarded the door of her bedroom, watching over her as she slept. Leaning back casually on the doorjamb, his arms were crossed across his broad chest as he stood tall, protecting the little angel he had grown to adore. But hearing a conversation in the nearby kitchen, he stepped away briefly from his position to listen.

"I think the party was a success, don't you Mare Bear?" GiGi asked, handing Mary freshly washed dishes, one by one, to dry.

"I would hardly call anything that I am a part of a success, Momma," Mary muttered, not interested in talking about an evening filled with the excitement of her sister celebrating a brand-new family while her own family was broken. "We offered the house, but Viv really did all the work…leaving us to clean up, as usual."

GiGi, still burned up at Sam, switched the subject. "Can I ask you a question?"

"As long as it has nothing to do with Philip or Wills or Viv's new foster kids…yes."

"All righty then…here goes. Do you think Sam is really all he's supposedly cracked up to be?"

"Ha! You're the one who set Viv up with the bearded cult man, so I've always thought you liked him. What's going on here?" Knowing her momma as well as she knew her own right arm, she darted her eyes at GiGi and demanded, "Spill the beans!"

"Well, I will…but first answer my question. Do you think Sam is all that? I mean, do you think he's good for Viv?"

Mary, having finished drying the last glass serving platter, squatted down to open a lower cabinet door. Gently placing the platter on an open shelf, she responded, "Hell to the no!"

"Oh, good Lord, Mary. I know you don't darken the doors of church anymore, but do you have to cuss like a sailor?"

Mary looked up at her mother, who had her hands planted firmly on her hips. Standing up again, she placed both her hands on GiGi's shoulders. "Mom," she said, her face only inches from her mother's face, "I think Sam Smith is in a cult. That is what I think. And now, thanks to the marriage that you arranged, my sister is in a cult. I broke free from it, remember? And it cost me dearly. But no…I don't think he is good for Viv at all, and I never will." She dropped her hands and turned to wipe down the kitchen counters.

"Well, he blew his top with me tonight. He went off on trying to censor what gifts I can give to Ruby and Rose, and I guess to Viv, too. Lately, I've been getting a bad vibe from him all the way around."

"A bad vibe, huh? Well, it's too little too late. We're all stuck with him now."

GiGi leaned over, resting her elbows on the counter. "Do you trust him?"

"I think I've made it clear that the only person I fully trust is Miss Charity, because she can't help but be who she is. There are no pretenses, no manipulative tactics… only the purest love comes from that kid. She is, in my mind, all that Sam Smith will never be, even on his best day."

"How about Tater Bug and Wills? Do you trust them?" she asked. "And how about me and your daddy…haven't we been here for you, honey?"

Pulling her hair down from the clasp that had held it on top of her head all evening, Mary answered, "Of course you've been here for me, and I adore Wills and Tate… but things change. Look at Wills now. Who would've dreamed our relationship would come to this? I've thrown him out of our home, Momma." Mary started to cry.

"You did what you had to do, honey." GiGi made her way over to Mary and hugged her tight. "With his unpredictable partying choices, Wills had become a liability for this family. One drinking and driving accident, God forbid, and a lawsuit could've taken this whole family down into the pit. You had to get him out, independent, and on his own before anything like that happened. Miss Charity, with all her needs, is going to require a lifetime of care, so she has to be our financial priority."

"I know. But don't you see? Even the people who are closest to me have changed. Wills...Philip...it makes me wonder who will be next. The only one who will not hurt me is the Little Miss. People let you down."

The conversation ended on that note with the words "people let you down" hanging in the air, perhaps traveling throughout eternity to shape not only Mary but others who are on the cusp of giving up. The angel tried to interfere, to stop Mary before she spoke the words into existence...before she spoke the negativity into her life and into her mother's life. But he was too late. The words had been spoken and would now do their work.

Chapter 6

Sunday mornings at church had become a time of refuge for Philip. Preacher Walker had initially guilted him into attending. Given the fact that the older pastor was faithful in visiting Philip each week, the guilt-trip worked. Over time, though, Philip had once again found his love for the church. His experience with the Lost Tribe Fellowship had turned him against God for a time, but eventually Philip faced the fact that his anger toward the Lord was not going to change anything. As he figured it, accepting God or rejecting Him made Him no less than completely God. Upon this epiphany, Philip decided he'd rather roll the dice on the side of God rather than on the side against God. That was how he rationalized it all and how he came to the point of allowing the church back into his life again.

On this particular Sunday, Philip's parents joined him. He no longer sat in the infamous "Montgomery family pew" as he had for so many years; instead, he now occupied a spot in the back row. His parents, devout Catholics, had decided to give the Baptist church a whirl for the sake of their son. Thinking of him going alone to worship God each week made them uncomfortable, sad, and a bit angry with Mary who had stopped going to church altogether. Sure, they were divorced, but Philip's parents believed they should still be married, as a family, to God.

As they got out of their car and began making their way toward the church building, Philip's mother, Agatha (whom everyone called Aggie), couldn't help but speak up. "You know, son, it wouldn't hurt for Mary to drag her lazy bones out of bed to bring Tate and Miss Charity to church every once in a while."

Expecting a response from Philip, Aggie was surprised to hear a shrill Southern squawk. "I know you're not talking about my daughter, Aggie. Even you wouldn't gossip on the Lord's day."

Philip turned to see that Poppy and GiGi had pulled in and parked several feet away. His mother and GiGi had attended school together from kindergarten straight through graduation, had competed against each other in every local pageant and every student council election, and had been co-captains of the cheerleading squad. They had put up with each other over the years for the sake of Mary, Philip, and the children, but everyone knew how much they secretly loathed each other.

Before GiGi married Poppy, she had courted Aggie's husband, who was at that time called Philip. Once Aggie got hold of him, however, he was known simply as "Pip." Philip had been named after his father and was thankful to *not* bear the same nickname. GiGi and Aggie, although grandmothers, were still as competitive as ever.

Aggie, not missing a beat, replied, "Get a clue, windbag. Gossip is when one tells an untruth, and as you know, I am all about the truth. Like that time I said you cheated to win student council president."

GiGi was just about to let her old rival have a good piece of her mind when Poppy shushed her. So instead she grabbed Poppy's arm and nearly took off in a slow jog, with her high heels clicking on overdrive to put herself in front of Aggie and Pip as they entered the church building. Jeannie, the pastor's wife, stood just inside the door with a smile that lit up the entire space. She customarily greeted each person with a hug or a handshake as they came in each week. Poppy shook Jeannie's hand, GiGi gave her a little pat on the back, and both took a bulletin.

Stealing a hasty glance back at her archnemesis, GiGi swiveled her head around and spoke before Poppy could shush her again. "Dear," she said, using the most Southern drawl she could muster, "I never had to cheat to beat you at anything…you were always runner-up to me. Heck, you even married my runner-up."

Poppy, aghast, yanked her into the sanctuary and down the aisle to their usual seat, which had been formerly

58

known as the Montgomery family pew but was now known as GiGi's pew. "What in God's name are you thinking, woman? Regardless of past differences, we share grandparenting duties with Pip and Aggie, so it would behoove us to get along with 'em."

GiGi, now seated, turned all the way around in the pew to stare Aggie down as she entered. "All bets are off with that deal now that Philip and Mary have called it splits." She bristled at the thought of Aggie calling her a cheater when it was Aggie's own son who had cheated on Mary. "I can't believe that woman had the nerve to come to *our* house for the party the other night. How dare she!" Spinning around to face the front, GiGi patted Poppy's leg and added, "Don't let it get your underoos all up in a wad that I called Pip my runner-up, either. He was never in the running for anything with me."

Preacher Walker was just about to take center stage to deliver the sermon he had prepared when Bonnie Cutless came walking in. Strolling down the aisle to take a seat right next to GiGi, fully expecting that to be the pew where Philip still sat, she made her way in, giving GiGi a slight wave of her hand with a look that said: "Yes…I'm back!" Preacher Walker, upon seeing her, motioned for the song leader to have the choir continue to sing so he could catch his breath. Jeannie had already filled him in on the near scuffle in the vestibule, and now this. He wondered if GiGi would be able to keep her big mouth shut. An extra verse or two of "Have Thine Own Way, Lord" would give the fireball some time to simmer down and might even speak to her heart. God was, hopefully, still in the miracle-working business.

GiGi, unnerved and horrified, immediately put her hand to her neck to check her pulse. And it was racing. Within seconds she had talked herself into full hyperventilation, and in nothing flat, she had laid herself out on the pew, feeling certain she was knocking at death's door. "Have Thine Own Way, Lord…Have Thine Own Way," she shouted. "Just come and take me home, Jesus. Aggie and

60

the skank sleazebag slut are both here eggin' me on this morning in this holy place, and I can't take it no more."

In the midst of the hoopla, someone had enough sense to call 911, and within minutes the woman who had shoved Aggie off her high horse just moments earlier had been carted off to the emergency room with what would later be identified as a panic attack.

The church service was cancelled, and upon leaving the building, Bonnie caught Philip's eye. "Hey, handsome," she said flirtatiously, making her way to him. "I thought you would've been sitting in the infamous 'Montgomery family pew' with your former nutcase mother-in-law this morning."

Philip, with full knowledge that everyone in the church knew about his affair with Bonnie, couldn't believe GiGi had called her out as a skank, sleazebag slut. And now she was calling him handsome? "Yeah, about that…I don't feel comfortable sitting with them since the divorce. They've been supportive of me and all, but I

61

don't want to be too pushy," Philip mumbled, hoping Bonnie would just walk on out of the church building.

"Well, if that's not the pot calling the kettle black, Philip. The old bird is about the pushiest creature on the planet, and I've seen a lot of pushy birds in my lifetime." Bonnie shook her head, recounting the embarrassing harangue that had occurred. "Personally, I hope she keels over today."

Finding herself in full agreement with Bonnie, Aggie spoke up. "I'm sorry, but I don't believe we've met."

Introducing his former lover to his parents was no easy feat, but Philip managed. As soon as they heard the name Bonnie and got a load of her tight-fitting dress and long, blond hair, they put two and two together. Philip, forced to own up to the full truth of his past now that his parents had moved back to town, had spilled the beans about his affair. "So," Aggie inquired, "are you a member of this church, Bonnie?"

"Actually, no…this is the first time I've attended in a very long time, which is probably why GiGi had a conniption fit." She laughed as she pictured the older woman dressed in her Sunday best laid out on the pew unable to catch her breath, telling Jesus to "take her home." "Don't worry, though, that woman won't die, because she's way too mean to die."

Aggie's eyes lit up as she listened to Bonnie slam the woman she had hated for as far back as she could remember. Suddenly, without any hint of warning, she grabbed her own neck and started poking fun. "I'm going home to be with Jesus, Poppy…" she mocked. "I think I can see the lights of glory!" No one wanted to laugh at her, but all who were standing nearby did. Her imitation of GiGi was spot on. She may have hated the woman, but she had spent a lot of time studying her every nuance. Even the way she threw her voice was a dead ringer for GiGi.

Bonnie couldn't help herself. She fell over onto a pew and giggled until she cried actual tears. "Do it again… please don't stop…I'd pay admission for this!"

And much to the chagrin of Pip, Aggie obliged. Prissing up and down the aisles, knocking on the ends of the wooden pews, she acted out the role of one she secretly hoped was now dead. "Hello? Jesus? Are you home? Your favorite Bible-toting believer is out here at the golden gate, ready to come in to order all the angels around about how things in heaven should be properly run." She kept it up and wouldn't stop no matter how many times Philip and his father implored her. "Oh, and as far as Aggie and Bonnie go, just strike their names off your Lamb's book of life list, because they aren't worthy of a mansion in glory the way I am." Years of pent-up anger burst from Aggie's seething mouth as she continued mocking. "You see, dearest Lord, I am a gentile Southern woman who has never sinned…I've never even let one drop of the devil's evil red wine touch my virgin lips, so I deserve to go to heaven…Jesus, let

Old Mona shed some bright light throughout the holy of holies by displaying all the special gifts you have lavished upon me. Ooooh, I am so humble. Just look at me…all humble pie with all my marvelous giftings."

Finally, Preacher Walker, who had been standing near the back door to shake hands with parishioners as they left, clued in to the spectacle that was now taking place in the sanctuary. "Aren't you Philip's mother?" he asked, interrupting Aggie's diatribe. "I don't believe I've seen you since I officiated Philip and Mary's wedding many moons ago."

Slightly embarrassed by the sudden appearance of the clergy, Aggie straightened her dress and responded, "Why, yes, Pastor, I am. It's so nice to see you again."

He looked around at those who had gathered to witness the reenactment of GiGi and smirked. "Do you know what my sermon was gonna be about today…I mean, had I had the chance to give it?"

No one answered. Like a kid caught with his or her hand in a cookie jar, they all looked plenty guilty.

"Well, I'll tell ya," he continued. "My message this morning, ironically, was gonna be on how we are supposed to love our neighbor. And as in the story of the Good Samaritan, as all you good church folk already know, sometimes your neighbor looks an awful lot like the people you don't associate with, or even the people you despise." He paused, looked up toward the pew where GiGi had nearly passed out, and added, "It sure is a good thing that each and every one of you knows the Lord Jesus and that you all love your neighbors and pray for your enemies as He has instructed you to do...yes, indeed, it is a mighty good thing."

Shaking Aggie's hand and then Pip's, he then quietly moseyed away, singing the old children's song:

> *Oh, be careful little mouth what you say,*
>
> *Oh, be careful little mouth what you say,*

For the Father up above is looking down with love,

So, be careful little mouth what you say.

The man had not only scored, but he had also made the extra point—his point and God's point.

Chapter 7

Ruby and Rose were sharp. In their brief time on earth, they had been around enough dishonest people to peg a hooligan in any group. Sam did not have them fooled, even though they both played the game by feigning gratefulness.

After the party, they had piled into the car and made their way to their new temporary home. The ride home was silent. Viv had tried to make some conversation with Sam, but he had not responded. The girls had lived through this scenario many times before and immediately knew this placement would not be a forever home. It would be just another stop.

Their shared room was nice. It was actually nicer than any they had ever been in. Viv had gone to great lengths to continue the princess theme into their little corner of the universe, which amounted to about two hundred square feet and a big window. White comforters covered in tiny pink rosebuds topped each twin-size bed, and twinkling lights hung from the ceiling, casting a glorious warm glow on the space. As instructed, both had put on their nightgowns and climbed into bed.

"This will be your nightly routine, girls," Sam had said, standing at attention in the doorway of their room. "Each evening, promptly at eight thirty, you are to be in your beds ready to hear a word from scripture." He had preached to them for thirty minutes as they fought to keep their eyes open. His spiel was about purity, about the proper way for a follower of Christ to dress and to speak, and about the many house rules. The girls didn't catch much of what he had to say, because they were worn-out. "The house rules will be listed on the refrigerator in the kitchen, and in the morning, you both will be required to sign the rules, indicating your agreement to comply." His face was stern, and the tone of his voice seemed to dare them to disobey.

Rose had interrupted him to remind him that while she could read and write a little, she was sure she would be unable to read a list of house rules. As for little Ruby, the poor dear wasn't able to read or write. Sam had taken this opportunity to explain that if they were to address him, a hand needed to be raised first. To speak, they must first be called upon. Ruby had then raised her own hand to ask if this was a school or a home, and that had infuriated Sam. It was a sincere question, but he had taken it as a sign of insubordination and had explained that defiance of the rules would result in a spanking with a paddle.

As Sam spoke, Viv looked on, offering the girls a warm smile. She was sending a message, nonverbally conveying that she was the nice one. But the girls didn't see a hateful man and a kind woman; instead, they looked upon the two and saw weakness. And to Ruby and Rose, weakness meant opportunity.

It wasn't on this first night that Rose decided she and her little sister would wreak havoc upon Viv and Sam, but it only took a matter of days for her to come to this conclusion. Each night, as she lay in bed listening to Sam berating Viv, calling her a worthless whore, reminding her that he would kill her before allowing her to divorce him, rage grew inside of her. He probably thought the girls were asleep or unable to hear his tirades, but he was mistaken. The two, pushed from pillar to post their entire lives, knew that the darkness of night exposed true relationships. To date, they had never been in a stable home, and in each home they had ever been a part of, nighttime always meant heated arguments and knockdown, dragged-out fights. In this particular home, the arguments started immediately, which likely meant it was more unstable than most.

"We need to disobey all their rules, do you understand me, Ruby?" No matter the rules, Ruby jumped into bed with her big sister each and every night. The two hid beneath the covers and whispered in secret.

71

"I don't want Sam to beat me," Ruby had explained, night after night, as Rose developed their strategic plan of action.

Rose didn't want to be spanked either, but she was bound and determined that Sam would *not* lord over her and her sister. "So, it's a beating? We've been hit so many times you should be used to it by now."

"It don't mean I like it, though." Ruby returned, considering how bad it would feel to be disciplined by a paddle.

Rose pulled her little sister in close and hugged her tight. "Do you remember the momma of the last house we lived at?"

"Yeah, she was mean." Ruby had been very afraid of the woman.

"Well, do you remember how she said my ass was like a concrete block?"

Ruby giggled because her sister had used the word "ass."
"Yep, I remember."

Tears welled up in Rose's eyes. "Why do you think she said that to me?"

"Because no matter how hard she whooped you, you never cried." Ruby admired her sister's strength and felt safe within her arms. Tears escaped from Rose's eyes, but Ruby didn't notice.

"I'm gonna tell you a secret, and if I do, will you promise to never tell a living soul?"

Ruby promised.

"My ass is not a concrete block at all. Every single lick that woman laid on me hurt really bad. I just chose not to cry, because I was not going to let her rule over me and my life. I used my mind to block out the pain."

Ruby, trying to process this secret, asked, "How do you block out a whoopin'?"

Rose, knowing Sam was going to be a tough nut to crack, had to teach her sister to become hard and tough. "I think about how much I hate momma and daddy for ditching us and about how much I hate all the foster parents who have beat us and cussed us and locked us in rooms and dumped us. I take all that hate, and I focus on it so hard that I don't even care about being hit. I have another secret, too; do you wanna hear it?"

"Yes, what is it?"

"There isn't really a Santa Claus, an Easter Bunny, or a God. It's all fake, Ruby…it's all made-up junk to try to control us kids. So you see? There's no reason to be good."

By this time, tears were streaming down Rose's face. Forsaken by everyone in her life save Ruby, she felt worthless and alone. Ruby began to cry, too. "Are you sure that Santa, the Easter Bunny, and God are all fakes?" she asked.

"You are four years old now," Rose answered. "It's time for you to know the truth and to be brave."

"Brave for what?"

"For the fight."

"What are we fighting for, Rose?" Ruby's voice was that of a four-year-old little girl. She spoke with a slight lisp as her words broke with sobs. Gentle as a lamb and unlike her older sister, Ruby was not born to be a warrior of any sort. Their meth addict mother had used during her pregnancy with Ruby, leaving the girl with a slight learning disability. People often called her "slow," which was not lost on Rose.

"You know what we're fighting for. I've told you thousands of times, so now it's time for you to tell me. But first, tell me who you are, little girl?" Rose kicked back the covers and grabbed a plastic princess crown from the nightstand, one that had been given as a gift at their party. Swiping away tears, she pulled Ruby up in the bed and plunked the crown on top of her head.

Ruby answered, "I'm Ruby."

Pointing to the crown, Rose repeated the question again. "Who are you, little girl?"

"I'm Princess Ruby?" Ruby asked, grinning while wiping away her own tears.

Rose smiled, proud of her sister. "That's right. You are Princess Ruby, and you have been captured by an evil man who is trying to make you a slave. But you aren't a slave, are you?"

"Is Sam the evil man?" Ruby asked, eyes as wide as saucers.

"Oh yes, he is the evilest of all evil men, and he wants you to be his slave instead of being the princess you were born to be. Are you going to give in and be his slave?" Rose prodded her sister down the path she knew she must go.

Ruby, on board with her sister now, answered quickly with glee, "No, I'm not a slave…I'm Princess Ruby!"

"And a princess is supposed to be treated like she's someone special, because you are very special. You deserve parents who are going to love you and take care of you, and I won't stop fighting until I find those parents. They are out there looking for you. Do you believe me?"

Ruby hung on to every word with hope. "Are my parents looking for you, too? Because you are my sister and that makes you a special princess, too."

Rose loved her sister so much at that moment that she feared her heart might burst. "Our new parents, once they finally find us, will love us both so much. They will never scream at each other, and they won't ever hit us. But they will always love you best of all."

"Why will they love me more?" the four-year-old asked, honestly wanting to know.

"Because you're perfect, Ruby. And when they find you, they will realize that they have found the most valuable treasure in the whole world. That's why your name is Ruby."

With that, Ruby leaped forward, grabbing her sister's neck with the tightest squeeze she could muster. "I'll take the whoopin', and I won't cry a bit. I promise, Rose, that I'll be a fighter like you."

"Good girl," Rose replied with a heavy heart, dreading all that her sister might be forced to endure. But it was for the best. If Rose was going to find proper parents for her sister, it would take a lot of work, a lot of disobeying, and a lot of spankings. The two girls would present a united front.

Chapter 8

Spring break on Panama City Beach had not been on Mary's wish list, yet there she was on the twelfth floor of a posh high-rise condo overlooking the pristine bluish-green Gulf. Anyone who knew the area also knew that Panama City Beach, at this time of year, was a haven for young adults looking to find alcohol, sex, and plenty of trouble. Days earlier, an excessively nosy GiGi had learned through a social media post that Wills was going to be spending the week in the party capital of the South and had made a split-second decision to book a condo. Her three-step plan was to spy on him, interfere if necessary, and keep him out of jail. Had GiGi not already paid for the trip before informing her about it, Mary might've said no. But it was a free trip. To the beach. So Mary had packed for Miss Charity and Tate, and they had headed south in a rented SUV with Viv and her foster daughters. Girls' trip or bust.

GiGi might have been a grandmother who was born a few years before the color television made its debut in America, but she had made herself a student of the computer, especially of all social media platforms. As soon as she learned she could find out any and all information within seconds utilizing the World Wide Web, the woman was all in. "From what I am seeing," she said, checking her cell phone, "there is a citywide party on the beach tonight where free alcohol is supposed to be flowing. I'd bet my bottom dollar that our young reprobate will be there boozin' it up." GiGi stalked her grandson's social media accounts like a woman gone mad, and though he had not posted anything about going to the event, she was betting on him being there. "I say Mary and I show up and bust that kid out of there."

"Wills is twenty-one, Mom—hardly a kid. He can drink himself into oblivion if that's what he chooses to do, and there's nothing you can do about it," Viv replied, ready to make the trip more about vacationing than digging up

80

dirt on Mary's prodigal. "How long has it been since you've seen boy wonder, anyway?"

"Five weeks, four days, two hours," and then looking down at her cell phone, she continued, "and twelve minutes. Who would've ever dreamed that our Wills would go all 'rogue deserter' on us?"

Mary, seated on the balcony braiding Tate's hair, could barely hear the conversation but caught the general gist of it. She called out, "You act like you're the only one this is affecting, Mom. How do you imagine Miss Charity is processing the fact that her brother dropped out of her life?"

"Excuse me, but he dropped out of my life, too," Tate added. Although she didn't talk about it much, Mary knew the situation had taken its toll on Tate. Wills had always been her hero, but over the past couple of years, he had really disappointed her.

***

Wills was on the beach when the party broke out, and he did have a drink in hand. Viv had volunteered to take care of the kiddos so her mother and Mary could go undercover to check up on the unsuspecting soul. Sitting in a couple of lawn chairs, wearing big, matching straw hats and sunglasses, the two spies-on-a-mission did their level best to remain incognito. When Wills went for his third and then for his fourth drink, however, GiGi broke her silence.

"Wills Montgomery," she squawked, alarming all the half-naked partiers nearby. "What in God's name do you think you're doing?" The old bird rose from her seat and stormed across the beach, sending particles of sand blowing in her wake as she trudged on toward her one and only grandson. Knocking the red cup out of his hand, she continued. "Pray tell, why have you forsaken your GiGi for this sin pit of lust and shame?"

Wills, tipsy and caught off guard, roared with laughter. "Oh my God! What are you doing here, crazy lady?"

Mary sat by watching, daring to hope that her son might decide to forget the party scene and join them in the condo for the week.

"Crazy lady?" she repeated, aghast. "I am your grandmother, and you will show me respect or I will wallop you right here in front of all these horny hellions who are headed to hell on a speedboat." Small in frame, GiGi looked like a mushroom beneath the huge straw hat. She jerked off her sunglasses to gain even more attention and eyeballed all the partiers who dared make eye contact with her before continuing. "Listen to me, you bunch of delinquent rabble rousers. If you don't get right with the Lord, He's gonna put you all on a shiny red speedboat and shoot you like a bullet through the ocean." She slapped her hands together and pointed out toward the Gulf of Mexico. "You are all gonna think you're in for the ride of your life, that you are on the fun boat, but those waters are gonna open up like the Bermuda Triangle and yank you all down to the fiery pit of hell. Just wait and see. You are playing a mighty dangerous game."

One of the partiers who heard GiGi's remarks began to chant: "We're all going to hell on a speedboat...we're all going to hell on a speedboat..." Within seconds, the chant had spread and was being broadcast across the beach area. The drummer of the band that was about to play picked up his sticks and began hitting his snare drum along with the beat of the chant. Wills turned and laughed at his GiGi, feeling cocky and full of himself.

"Go back home to your sanctimonious life," he said, sneering at his grandmother. "You kicked me out of your life, remember?" Spotting his mother seated nearby, he made sure she saw him shake his head at her. "All of you need to stay out of my life. If I go to hell, then I go to hell...don't worry about it." He then turned his back on them and joined in on the chant, walking toward the massive throng of untamed, rowdy kids. A topless girl donning bright-yellow string bikini bottoms ran to him.

Wills scooped her up as she threw her legs around his waist, kissing him on the mouth.

"That's the limit, Wills Montgomery! Do you hear me? You are officially going to hell!" GiGi hollered.

But he walked on toward the masses, propping the girl up around his hips with his hands.

"I see your hands on her butt, Wills! And I can also see her bare boobies, son! My heart is racing! Do you hear me? Your GiGi may be having a heart attack right here in sin city."

Wills had sent a strong message, and the message had been received.

***

By the time Mary and GiGi made it back to the condo, they were beat. The traffic in Panama City was bumper to bumper, and it had taken a full hour to drive fifteen miles.

Viv had ordered pizza, and the girls were happily chowing down when they arrived, looking haggard.

"Well," Viv started, "I can take one look at you two and tell how things went at the party. The drunk is drunk, am I right?"

"Shut up, Viv, or I'll slap you down and send you to hell right with Wills. I brought you into this world, and I will take you out." GiGi was over it.

Viv, ever the boss, reminded her mom, "If you kill me, I'll go to heaven because I am saved just like you. Contrary to what you may tell yourself, you don't hold the market on God and heaven."

Viv knew better than to engage her mother at a time like this, but she had gone and jumped into the fray anyway. So her mother unleashed the hurt she felt toward Wills at her daughter. "You are doing the devil's bidding in that cult, and it's high time you got a clue. If I murder you for being such a big-mouth sassy pants, you will bust the gates of hell wide open. It's a fact. Read your Bible. Anyone who is in a cult is doomed for hell. The good book says it."

"Well, at least my husband's penis isn't being passed all around Cleveland, Tennessee." Viv had thrown out a jab, a strange and unexpected jab, and GiGi fired back.

"Are you saying your daddy is having an affair? Is that what you're trying to say, Viv?" GiGi put her finger up to her neck to check her pulse. "We may be calling an ambulance, Mary, and you are my prime witness. Your cult-seeking sister is trying to kill me with murderous words!"

Viv rolled her eyes, acting like she wasn't about to unleash something that would change their lives forever. But she knew it would. "Blah, blah, blah...I'm talking about Philip's penis."

Tate, sitting at the counter eating pizza, jerked up. "What are you saying, Aunt Viv? Stop it!"

The stress of living with Sam and of putting up with GiGi's constant barbs had gotten to her. On any normal day, Viv wouldn't have been so careless. "I'm sorry, Tater Bug. I wasn't even thinking about you and the girls sitting here."

Chapter 9

No one was more shocked than Philip Montgomery. The picture was real, it was circulating all over town, and it was definitely his penis. The bottom part of his face, unfortunately, had made it into the photo, too, which made denying the snapshot an impossibility. But where had the image come from? Who had taken it? Why? And how? The man had been through enough drama over the past few years of his life to create a successful soap opera, but this was over the top.

Mary had called and chewed him out. He'd assured her that he had not slept with anyone, had not posed for a nude photo, and had never made a sex tape. However, his ex-wife was looking at the proof right before her eyes.

"Chief, I mean, that's your penis," she had said.

Chief…Mary hadn't called him that in months. She'd been crying, he could tell.

"Do you know what this is going to do to Tate? Lord…a picture of her daddy's penis is being passed around by all her friends," she continued. "She's already getting messages about it."

Who would send a message to a teenage girl about her father's penis picture? The Lord's people. Apparently, friends from her church youth group and her Christian homeschool tutorial class were on top of the issue. Their texts were full of offers to pray for her and for her family, but even Tate could see through it. Those kids were enjoying the hype at her expense.

Philip had tried to calm Mary down, but truth be known, the man himself needed someone to calm *him* down. This was, after all, *his penis* that was being passed around for everyone to see.

"Thank God my man parts aren't small…you know?" he had joked, trying to bring some levity into the conversation. Mary, though, had not found his words humorous. After a few choice words, which included a comment about cutting his penis off and feeding it to Trudy, their dog, she had hung up. All the hope he'd allowed himself to kindle in his heart about reuniting with his first love was now gone. Mary would never see him as a victim in this and would never trust him again.

Preacher Walker came as soon as Philip called. The whole idea of pictures being shared by messages on a cell phone was foreign to him. Philip, to show his elder how it worked, took a picture of the two of them together and then sent it to the pastor's phone. When the white-haired man received it, he understood.

"Have you lost all your ever-lovin' God-given sense, son?" the pastor asked, putting two and two together in his mind and realizing that the whole town had now seen way too much of Philip. "Why would you ever allow anyone to take a picture of your private parts? Or did you take it? Heavens to Betsy, please tell me you didn't take a picture of your penis, because that would be just plain sick."

"I'm telling you, Preacher, I didn't take that picture and have never allowed anyone else to take a picture of my man parts; I would never do something like that." Philip wrung his hands one minute and dragged his hands through his hair the next. He was as nervous as a man with a comb-over in a windstorm.

The pastor, seeing Philip's anxiety, sought to have a real conversation with him. "You're telling me this picture of your man parts is out there, with part of your face in it, and you have no idea who took it or who would pass such a thing around? I think it's safe to say that Mary would never do a thing like this." The old man started pacing the floor the more he thought about it. This news would rock his church congregation to the core. How would he explain it away? He couldn't ignore it, that was for sure.

"It looks like the picture was taken in the bed I have here at the office, so it must have been recent. I've been thinking that someone broke in while I was sleeping and took it."

"So you're saying someone broke into this place, stripped you down naked, took a picture, dressed you up in your pajamas again, and then left without you having a clue?" The older man was trying to talk through this fiasco with Philip, but his sarcasm was evident.

"I sleep naked," Philip admitted, feeling a bit chagrined. "So someone must've broken in and snapped the picture while I was sleeping."

"Someone who knew you sleep naked?"

"Maybe. I don't know."

The exchange between the two on such a sensitive subject was awkward. Preacher Walker, who had been aimlessly walking about the room, stopped on a dime and snapped at Philip. "Do I look like a complete idiot to you? What in Sam's hill would somebody do something like that for?" The man was infuriated. "Glory, son, you are gonna have to come clean on this and repent. It's the only way."

"I can tell you think this all sounds nuts, but there is no other explanation."

The pastor laughed out loud, and it wasn't the sort of laugh indicating that he was anywhere near happy. "Nuts? No, I wouldn't call it nuts, Philip. This is going to be the final nail in the coffin with you and Mary. She won't get over this." He started pacing again, shaking his head in a fretful way. "And then there's Tater and Wills, who are going to be humiliated forever. You just don't move on from this sort of thing, Philip. It's your penis in plain view for the world to see."

No one believed Philip. Why would they? Every possible theory he came up with sounded harebrained, even to him. Plenty of women had come on to Philip since the divorce, but he had not shown any interest in any of them. None of them had been invited into his bedroom, that was for sure. Had he offended one of them enough that she would want revenge? Surely not. He was a middle-aged man with half-grown kids, not a young buck with a lot to offer. He definitely was not worth someone going out on this kind of limb for.

Then there was the business side. When the scandal of his affair with Bonnie had broken, along with the news of his dabbling in the occult, many of his lessors had been forced to relocate. The townspeople, in an effort to teach Philip a lesson, had refused to frequent any commercial property owned by him for a very long time. It was what had nearly forced the man into bankruptcy. As a result, a few of the businesses didn't recover. Maybe one of those former business owners had caught wind of him getting back up on his feet again with his business and had felt there was a score to settle. Could any of them be this underhanded?

Bonnie, of course, had also crossed his mind. At one time, she had stepped over into "certifiably crazy town," but now she appeared to have it together. She had mentioned she was in a relationship with someone, but not her husband, of course. If she was involved with another man, she would have no interest in doing something like this to him. Not to mention, she had arranged leases on most of his available property and had been a real salvation to him. While for selfish reasons he hoped against hope that this was not Bonnie's doing, he decided to call her. He needed to know.

She picked up after only one ring. In the past, she had always let the phone ring three full times. It was one of those weird things she'd overcome since her time at the mental health center.

"Hello? Philip? Lord, I was hoping you'd call."

"You were?" he asked, caught off guard.

"Yes, Chief, your penis is being splashed all over town, and I'm sure you understand that this is an emergency." She knew calling him Chief was off-limits, but given his dire situation, what could he say? "My boss has been calling me nonstop and is outraged since he just leased many of your properties in the hopes of an aboveboard, respectable relationship. You and your private man parts have put me in a horrible situation with him."

Bonnie seemed really upset, which threw Philip off-balance a bit. He had called to question her about whether she had taken the photo, and yet she was unloading on him.

"Is he thinking about breaking the contract? I don't think that would be legal, would it?" Philip stumbled over his words, clearly unprepared for the turn this conversation was taking.

"I don't know that he cares about the legality of it all as much as he cares about his business and reputation. You have created a big mess with your junk." Bonnie was in full lecture mode. "What were you thinking Philip? Were you drunk or something?"

It didn't take very long for Philip to figure out that Bonnie's new flame was her boss and that she was definitely not the one behind the irreverent photo of his manhood. She said she believed him when he told her it was all a setup, but he wasn't too sure if she really did. No one else believed his story. Bonnie also promised to talk her boss, her lover, off the cliff. He knew her wild, imaginative ways and assumed if anyone could make the man forget about the penis photo, it was her. For a moment, he let his mind go back to relive his past with her. But it was only for a moment.

Chapter 10

Viv was in the grocery, minding her own business. The week had been difficult. Most people would never understand what it was like to live with an abusive husband and two young trauma kids. But Viv, ever keeping up the ruse, carried a look that said all was perfect in her corner of the world. When her ex-boyfriend approached in the frozen food section, Viv just about choked on the mint she was sucking. Their eyes met, and she decided not to be the first to speak. Offering a slight grin, she passed him by.

"Viv," he called out, the familiar sound of his voice causing the hair on her neck to rise to attention, "aren't you going to speak to me?" He laughed. She had passed him by and could've easily continued to walk, pretending not to hear him. But her body didn't cooperate with her heart. And she turned.

As the two ex-loves talked nonchalantly about life, Michael had no clue that just that morning she had been shoved into a wall by the man she had married and that, in the process, he had grabbed her hair and yanked it down hard. Her shoulder might present an outward bruise over the next few days, but her worn and tattered soul was already bruised. As for her head, it was missing a handful of hair.

"How's Katie?" she asked, trying to make conversation, unaware that she was running her fingers through her hair, absentmindedly looking for the area where Sam had yanked it out.

At one time, Viv had loved Michael with all her heart. They had dated throughout high school and, to her knowledge, had never exchanged a single harsh word. He had treated her as a princess, with utmost respect. But he was part of the Catholic Church, which was different from Viv's own Southern Baptist roots, so unbeknownst to the brutally handsome man standing before her in the frozen food section of the local Cooke's Food Store, he had never passed muster with GiGi. From the moment they had started dating, her mother had been working against him.

After the breakup with Viv, Katie, a girl Michael had met in college, swooped in. "Haven't you heard?" he asked. "She filed for a divorce a few months ago."

Viv was stunned. Having had such a difficult time finding anyone who could replace Michael in her own life, she'd remained single for many years before settling for the man who was now beating her on a daily basis. "I am so sorry, Michael," she managed, holding back the urge to hug him. "What happened?"

Of course the question was nosy, but this was Viv's way. Michael knew it and didn't seem to mind. "Can you believe the contractor who was heading up the new addition of our house was more appealing than me?" He held up his biceps, showing off his muscles as he spoke.

"Oh God! That tramp cheated on you?" Viv exploded, not even attempting to hold her anger in. "Well, if she's that type of a person, she never deserved you in the first place."

Michael, surprised by her reaction, instinctively reached out and touched her hand as it rested on the shopping buggy. "Hey, listen," he insisted, his voice soft and reassuring. "I'm doing OK." His eyes sparkled as he spoke. Viv had always crushed on those darned baby blues. He continued. "Katie and I didn't have the happiest marriage, and we are both to blame for that. I'm not sure we ever loved each other in the first place...but she's definitely not a tramp. The guy with the tool belt just offered her the attention she wasn't getting from me."

"He offered to hammer her, you mean?" Viv quipped, still fuming.

Michael couldn't help but laugh. Viv had always been quick-witted and full of energy. They chatted for a few

102

more minutes, and then he asked for her cell phone number. She rattled it off to him without any thought or hesitation as they parted ways, and she dared to hope that she'd hear from him right away.

Even though the two lived in the same small town, incredibly this was the first time they'd seen each other since their break up. He had finished his bachelor's and master's degrees out of state and had even worked an internship in that same area before returning home. In her eyes, the years had been good to him. As if it were possible, her first and only love had become even more handsome.

As Viv walked away from Michael, her heart raced and her hands shook. She knew the reason why. As long as she could remember, even during the years they'd dated as teenagers, he had always triggered that type of reaction in her. When his hand had touched hers, Viv felt her whole world shift. She abhorred the long stupid skirt she was wearing as much as the doily on her head, but more than anything, she loathed Sam Smith, her abuser. And as for the demon kids, Ruby and Rose, she wouldn't give them a second thought if they walked out of her life the next day. Those girls were driving her mad. Earlier that morning, Viv had found every one of her pumps in the bathtub. Each had been garnished with urine. Stinking urine! The girls had taken turns peeing inside them at some point during the night or early morning. In addition, during the time they'd been in her home, they'd peeled random pieces of wallpaper off of the walls, stuffed random things down the toilets to stop them up, painted their bedroom walls with feces, and scratched frowning faces into the dining room table. Their strange behavior had become the norm, and it was all too much.

Michael had just removed the blinders from her eyes. The cult was out, and a steamy love affair was in. If Viv could figure a way to freedom, those baby blue eyes would belong to her once again. She would stop at nothing to achieve her ends. There was no way Michael could be prepared for what was coming to him. A woman kept under the authoritative thumb of an abusive husband, when given the opportunity for a safe escape, could be someone mighty interesting to handle. The woman would give everything to him if he asked.

Chapter 11

When GiGi, Mary, Viv, and Jeannie met for lunch at the local Jenkins Restaurant, they expected to enjoy fresh, homemade chicken salad on buttered toast with the best chili in town, but as with any group of Southern females, rarely does anything go as planned.

"OK girls," GiGi began, "I have seen Philip's penis. God, I tried to avoid it, but a member of my Sunday school class, who shall remain unnamed, sent it to me over text. I didn't even know what it was until I blew it up on my cell phone screen." Before taking a break for air, she added, "Mary, that mole on the end of his thing-a-ma-jig really needs to be checked out by a professional. It is sort of shaped like the head of Mickey Mouse, which could mean cancer…and that's all I'm saying on the subject."

Jeannie, who was swallowing a big bite of her chili, just about choked. "Are you kidding?"

"I couldn't agree more, Jeannie! What is your deal, Mother?" Mary, feeling rather appalled, had butted in with enough heat to sizzle the freshly dyed hair on her momma's head. "How could you bring a thing like this up in a public place? And around Jeannie, who happens to be Preacher Walker's wife?"

Jeannie giggled. "I may be married to a preacher, Mary, but I'm no prude. I've actually seen a penis or two in my lifetime." The woman was a pistol, a true match for anything GiGi could ever dish out. "And for your information, Mary, while I don't mind your mother talking about Philip and his penis business…what does bother me is not knowing who the unnamed source of that text to your momma is." Then, turning toward GiGi, she added, "Go ahead and squawk, you old buzzard. Who is spreading that penis photo around our church?"

As the two old friends bantered back and forth, Jeannie prodding and GiGi refusing to give up her source, Mary sat in disbelief. Even though she wasn't married to Philip any longer, as far as her family and friends were concerned, she was still tied to him. His penis was therefore her penis.

GiGi, believing the only way to keep her daughters honest was to keep them on their toes, decided to stoke Mary's fire a bit more. "Jeannie," she said, "would you like to see Philip's mole? You know, just to give an opinion on whether it's skin-cancer doctor worthy."

Jeannie, catching on very quickly to what GiGi was up to, couldn't help but laugh. "You know I don't want to see that thing, especially if it has a Mickey Mouse mole," she shot back. "I think that might ruin Disney for me for good, and I've lived a long life loving old Mickey Mouse."

Mary didn't think her mother or Jeannie were humorous at all. Why did they have to torture her? Every time the two hens got together, it seemed they cackled more and more. "Can we change the subject to Viv? Is anyone else noticing that the big mouth hasn't said a word the whole time we've been here?"

GiGi had indeed noticed and was not planning to leave her other daughter out.

Fingering her sandwich like it was some sort of rare Cuban cigar, she sniffed it loudly enough for everyone to notice. "Mmmmm, don't you love a good chicken salad sandwich, Viv?" she asked.

Viv, looking down her nose at her mother for acting like a goof, countered, "Why in God's name are you sniffing that sandwich? Eat it already."

"I wonder if this chicken came from the frozen food section at Cooke's Grocery," GiGi added, just before taking a big bite from her sandwich. She chewed slowly, watching her daughter's eyes, waiting for a reaction. But Viv, accustomed to her mother's annoying barbs, refused to engage. So GiGi continued. "Mary, have you heard the news? I'm sure Viv has heard it by now. It seems that Catholic Michael is getting a divorce."

"Viv's Michael?" Mary asked, surprised by the news but equally surprised about the subject of Michael being brought up. "Listen, if you're wanting to set me up with Michael, I am not interested. His blond hair and blue eyes were always Viv's thing…not mine."

Viv still sat quietly, her eyes boring a hole through her mother's face.

"Sugar, you've already heard the news, am I right?" GiGi asked pointedly.

Viv, who had been secretly texting Michael over the past few weeks, decided to be honest. Obviously, one of her mother's goons had seen her and Michael talking at the grocery store and had reported it. "Yes, I ran into Michael at Cooke's a few weeks ago, and he told me the news…but you didn't have to play a juvenile game with me, Mother. You could've just asked me."

Mothers know their children better than anyone else, and GiGi was no exception. She knew Viv and Mary as well as she knew the back of her hand, and she knew full well that her blabbermouth daughter would have spilled the beans about running into Catholic Michael at Cooke's Food Store, and especially about his impending divorce, unless she had information to hide. Viv was up to something, and GiGi wasn't going to let it go.

"Jewel Disharoon saw you two chatting it up at Cooke's, and she said you and Catholic Michael looked awfully happy to see each other. Did you tell Sam about seeing your ex?" GiGi threw the question out on the table like she'd thrown the two empty packets of sugar she'd added to her already sweetened tea. Jeannie and Mary, clearly not overthinking the exchange, continued eating as they listened.

Viv's face became flushed; she could feel it. Whenever she became angry or anxious, her ears would turn bright red and would burn. As she felt them heating up, she despised her genetic makeup. That particular trait she had inherited from her mother of all people, who was seated across from her taking note.

"Why would I tell Sam about seeing Michael?" Viv retorted. "My past is where it belongs…in my past."

GiGi, noticing Viv trying to hide her bright-red ears, turned from teasing to concerned. "Viv, honey, is everything all right between you and Sam?"

"Of course, what kind of question is that?" Viv answered with a big smile, working to hide the truth.

The question had been GiGi's barometer, and Viv's answer told her everything she didn't want to hear. Something had gone awry with Sam Smith and her daughter. The old bird would have to get to the bottom of it.

Chapter 12

It had been several weeks since she'd heard from Wills, much less seen him, so dropping Miss Charity off with Sam didn't seem like a bad idea. Sam told her that Viv was making a quick run to the grocery store and assured Mary he wouldn't be left alone with the little girl who proudly bore the extra chromosome for very long. This was, after all, an emergency.

Tate and GiGi rode with her. They took off toward Chattanooga to look for Wills in an apartment complex where he'd been spotted drunk and passed out on the sidewalk the night before. Phone calls had been traded and texts passed along, and finally word had found Mary. She had called Philip to report the news and had promised to update him as her search went on. They both were slow to face the truth that Wills's drinking binges were out of control.

Rose and Ruby were home with Sam too, kept in their usual spot that was saved for those times when Viv was away. Being locked in a storage closet wasn't so bad once you got used to it, at least that's what the girls kept telling each other. They had been treated much worse at other homes, and keeping secrets was as much a part of their story as were the scars on their legs…the ones put there by their last foster mother who used a paring knife as a primary form of discipline.

Miss Charity had only known love in her lifetime, so when she was thrown in with the two foster girls, she thought it was a game. Hugging both Rose and Ruby, she giggled when they shoved her away. The girls were determined not to let anyone into their hearts, even a little girl in pigtails who had special needs. After some time had passed, Miss Charity became bored. Her friends weren't playing with her, and the closet didn't have toys or music, so she started to knock on the door. When Sam didn't answer, she banged louder. Rose and Ruby, huddled together in a corner, watched closely, knowing the girl bearing the extra chromosome was breaking one of Sam's many rules. If they were quiet in the closet, he agreed not to tie them up and gag them.

"We should tell her to stop banging," Ruby urged Rose, "or he might tie all three of us up."

Rose, considering her sister's concern, shushed Miss Charity and, in return, received a big hug and a kiss on her cheek. Rose quickly wiped away the saliva. "Gross! Who raised you? A bunch of animals?"

"Did she lick you?" asked Ruby.

"I think she did," replied Rose, still wiping her face with the sleeve of her shirt. "That kid is nasty."

Ruby liked Miss Charity. Every time she'd been around her, Miss Charity had been all smiles and giggles. "She isn't nasty at all," replied Ruby. "I think she just wants to be our friend." Ruby reached out her hand for the girl in pigtails, and in return, Miss Charity grasped her hand tightly. "See, Rose? She likes me, and I think she likes you, too."

Rose huffed, rolling her eyes.

Miss Charity was nonverbal and therefore was unable to express her thoughts, feelings, and emotions with words, but she was a master at showing love and joy through her actions. And she clearly understood that the girls were harmless. Upon Ruby's defense of her, she shot a huge grin toward Rose and held out her other hand for Rose to take.

"Listen, kid," Rose said in a whisper, "we aren't your cousins, and we're not your friends. We're foster kids just trying to survive. You don't want us or need us in your life, OK?"

Miss Charity allowed her smile to linger and refused to draw back her hand. Finally, Rose took it into her own hand. "You have Down syndrome, Miss Charity, and I'm not exactly sure what that is, but I know it doesn't make you very smart. You probably don't understand that your Uncle Sam is a very bad man. He will hurt you. He'll hurt all three of us if we're not very, very quiet." Rose's voice was laced with anxiety. Even though she had told Ruby she wasn't afraid of Sam, it was evident that she was very afraid. "Please don't make another sound, OK?"

As Rose tried to help Miss Charity understand the predicament they were in, Ruby stood by nodding her head. Miss Charity didn't understand. She couldn't. For to her, no one was to be feared. After the girls shushed her one last time, Miss Charity turned and banged on the door again. It opened.

"Oh great," muttered Rose.

Sam had duct tape in his hand.

Chapter 13

GiGi sent a text to Viv, explaining the plight of Wills and their rescue attempt. Viv was with Michael. It was the first time they'd met, and she'd driven to the Charleston, Tennessee, exit, about fifteen minutes away, to meet him on a private gravel road. She had joined him in his pickup, where he had three sacks of groceries waiting on her. They had talked, held hands, and even kissed, but that was as far as things had gone.

It has often been said that it only takes a slight spark to rekindle an old flame, and that was proving true for Viv. The many times she had been mocked and cut to the core by Sam had left her empty. Over and over again, he had called her ugly and a whore, had told her she was worthless, selfish, a nag, and a bore. He'd made bruises on her arms but had left gaping wounds in her heart. Michael had not done much of anything. He had texted Viv after seeing her at Cooke's Food Store but not with any expectations. He'd simply been kind. And when someone is hurting and hiding a secret, kindness is not only a healing balm for the soul but a fragrant incense, breathing new life into the dark, barren spaces.

Viv, in response, had gushed over Michael through text. She'd called him strong, sensitive, and handsome, and made him feel worthy. His divorce had left him quite empty, and Viv's words brought much-needed restoration back into his hurting heart. The longing to be together had become so strong that Viv became willing to take the chance of being caught. And so they had met, and the physical attraction now left them both feeling more alive than they could ever recall feeling before. They planned to meet only twice a month until Viv could figure a way out of her abusive marriage, but both knew they wouldn't hold to it. They also agreed to hold off on sex until she was divorced, but that was another rule made to be broken. Many years had passed since the two had dated, but now it was as if they had never been apart. Viv was actually in love.

On the ride back to her house, Viv had received the text from her mother about the hunt for Wills. Not wanting to return home to Sam and the girls, she made a quick call to tell her husband she needed to drive to Chattanooga to help find Wills. When he didn't answer, she left a brief message and then dialed Michael.

At the same time, Mary, GiGi, and Tate were on the verge of finally locating Wills, who was believed to be somewhere on campus at the University of Tennessee in Chattanooga. They had been blatantly asking around, unafraid of offending anyone who might be put off by their candid questions and remarks. Finally, after badgering dozens of college-aged adults, a young woman had told them where they could likely find the prodigal son. She had referred to herself as a friend of Wills, which sent GiGi into orbit. "You're telling me that you are a friend of my grandson, Wills Montgomery?" she'd asked with a tone, Mary and Tate standing behind her. "I have a tough time swallowing that pill, honey."

"Really? Because we are very good friends." The girl's voice was raspy and hard, probably from leading a life that was far from innocent. She continued, coyly leading her older counterpart on. "He dated one of my besties not too long ago, and that's how we met. Once he laid eyes on me, I'm sure he wished he'd met me first. We would've had a good time, if you know what I mean." The young woman, smoking a cigarette, had blown smoke directly into GiGi's face as she spouted off the last few words.

"You look like you've spent one too many days at an outdoor hippie-filled music festival, and yes, I do know what you mean since I obviously wasn't born yesterday. But let's get to the point…you wanted to seduce my grandson with your sexual wiles and then get him hooked on nicotine, didn't you?" GiGi, rapidly fanning the smoke away with both of her hands, was too caught up in the moment to stay on her original course, which was to figure out *where* Wills could be found. Words rattled out of her mouth like coins falling from a slot machine that had hit five cherries in a row. "You are covered in more tattoos than a sailor from World War II, your hair looks like it hasn't been washed or brushed in your entire lifetime, your clothes don't match, and you are not wearing shoes…" She took a deep breath before continuing. "Not to mention that you are smoking a cigarette and drinking a beer in the middle of the day. And yet you *say* you are a friend of *my* sweet angel boy? Wills Montgomery? The boy I saw baptized when he was only ten years old? I guess I've left the planet and have officially entered the twilight zone."

The young woman howled with laughter. She actually found GiGi's honest disgust of her to be both funny and refreshing. "Listen, Grandmaw, do you want to have a seat and get to know me? Cause I'll buy you a beer and offer you a smoke if you're interested, and then we can talk about the twilight zone. When I'm smoking weed, I sometimes feel like I'm floating around in space, too." She giggled, took a swig from her bottle of beer, and added: "See? We've got lots in common."

It dawned on GiGi, as she snapped back into reality following Mary's pinch on her behind, that she wasn't there to redeem the wicked from their sins but to find her grandson. Fortunately for them, the sassy girl with the pack of Marlboros and a Bud Light was willing to talk. Within minutes, they had arrived at the campus apartment she'd suggested.

Mary demanded to be the one to go knock on the apartment door and confront Wills, while leaving GiGi in the car to wait with Tate, but Tate asked her mother to stay with her. The whole situation made her uneasy. As a result, GiGi was the one who knocked on the door.

After the discussion she'd had with Wills's "friend," she was plenty wound up when the door opened. "Where in the name of Sam Pete is my grandson? You tell me now, or I'm calling the cops. Just try me."

The twenty something young man who stood before her wore boxer shorts. That's all he had on. GiGi didn't notice. "Get out of my way," she barked, shoving him to the side and pushing her way into the dank apartment. "Wills, darling, where are you?" she called out.

"Ma'am, I'm pretty sure you can't just barge into my apartment. I think it's trespassing or something." The guy in the boxer shorts, still standing by the open door, spoke in a monotone and was very deadpan about the whole incident.

GiGi, in response, roared, "Shut up, stoner! I know your type. You've been holed up here in this apartment snorting your cocaine and smoking your pot. You're trying to send my grandson to hell on the back of the pink unicorns you probably see while you're high as a darned kite, but I won't let you do it!"

The young man quickly discerned that he might be dealing with a crazy lady, so he obliged. "Wills Montgomery is asleep in the next room. Is that who you want to beat the hell out of?"

She thought for a moment, took a deep breath, calmed down a bit, and answered, "Yes, bring Wills Montgomery out here to me. I do want to beat the ever-loving hell out of him."

Chapter 14

Having your feet and hands bound by duct tape wasn't so bad by Miss Charity's estimation, but the slap across her face hurt really bad. Her lip had pouted, and in response he had screamed something at her, asking her if she wanted another slap or a good beating. Of course she didn't want another slap or a beating and couldn't figure out why Sam was so angry. Several minutes had passed, and her cheek was still fiery red. Ruby and Rose, sitting on the floor next to her with their knees up under their chins, felt sorry for the little girl who had special needs. Though they were young, they knew she lacked the ability to comprehend abuse on any level. And although they wanted to offer comfort, they wouldn't dare because Sam had threatened to tie them up if they as much as lifted a finger to loosen the tape that bound Miss Charity.

Having Down syndrome is both a blessing and a curse. On one hand, these special angels never have to battle envy, bitterness, greed, or the all-too-destructive pit of self-love. That extra chromosome typically adds up to an extra measure of love, joy, and acceptance. On the other hand, though, self-defense for these individuals is nearly nonexistent. Unable to grasp the depravity of humanity, they can be targeted by predators without ever knowing it until it's too late. In Miss Charity's case, being nonverbal left her with an even a bigger disadvantage. Due to her small frame and lack of muscle coordination, not only could she not defend herself, but she could never verbally report what had happened to her. If anyone was ever to find out about her being abused in that closet by her Uncle Sam, it would be up to Rose or Ruby.

"Her fingers are turning blue," whispered Ruby. "That's not good, is it?"

"Shhh," Rose answered quietly. "She'll be fine."

While Miss Charity's disability was evident because of her almond-shaped eyes, her lack of communication skills, her small stature, and the zipper scar on her chest, Ruby and Rose had their own invisible disability. It is normal for babies to be nurtured, held, and cared for, but these two girls had never had the opportunity to become attached to anyone. Born to a meth addict, they had been left in a pack and play from birth to fend for themselves, and it wasn't until their mother was arrested that they'd made their way into the foster care system. But foster care had not been much better. Almost everyone they'd been placed with had been in it for the money, not for the girls' welfare. Neglect and abuse were the cornerstones their lives had been built upon, which had caused their minds to be wired differently. They felt normal, but their actions on any given day proved otherwise.

"But what if Sam hurts her real bad and she has to go to the hospital?" Ruby asked, not giving up.

Rose, protecting the only person she loved, pressed her hand over Ruby's mouth. "I told you, we have to be quiet or he will tie us up, too. I'm sorry Miss Charity has Down syndrome, but she isn't one of us."

Rose looked over toward Miss Charity, who looked confused and afraid. She continued. "My only job in life is to keep you safe; I can't take on anybody else."

Rose removed her hand from her sister's mouth, and Ruby started to cry. "But I like her," she said.

Before she could continue her thought, the door of the closet swung open again. This time Sam was holding a paddle. "Was that your voice I just heard in here, Ruby?" He had been standing right outside of the door. "Did you not hear me say that there should be no talking? Yet you disobey me?"

Sam was furious.

"No, Sam," Rose interrupted, frightened by the look in his eyes. "I was the one talking, and I'm really sorry.

Please forgive me." She sounded sincere. Manipulation was her game, and the girl played it well.

Ruby couldn't let her big sister get a beating for her; it had happened too many times in the past. So she screamed, "No! It wasn't Rose! You're right, Sam, it was me! I was talking!"

Sam, looking back and forth between the girls, was deciding whom he would beat with the wooden paddle. Truth be told, he was probably going to end up beating both of them for good measure, so it was more of who he would beat first. Rose, not new to this type of punishment, knew Sam's type and summed up fairly quickly that Sam could potentially decide to paddle all three of them. So she did something very brave and selfless.

"Good thing Ruby is trying to cover up for me, because what I was saying just before you opened the door and showed your ugly-ass face was that you're nothing but a wolf in sheep's clothing."

Ruby gasped. Her sister had used a curse word, which was one of the many rules she wasn't allowed to break in Sam and Viv's home. In other foster homes, expletives were allowed and even encouraged, but not in this one.

"That's right, you sorry stinking piece of shit!" she continued, ranting. "I know a fake when I see one, and you're a big, fat ugly fake who is going to burn in hell when you die!"

Rose was fully aware she was unleashing a dragon, but it was her way. To protect her sister, she would take the full brunt of Sam's anger. Only this time, it didn't work. The brutal man, seeing right through Rose's intentions, grabbed Ruby, yanked her pants down to her knees, and hit her bare bottom over and over and over again. To punish Rose. To seek vengeance. To take them all by surprise and to hurt them at the deepest level possible. Ruby shrieked. A couple of times, she instinctively reached her hand back to protect herself, only to find the wooden panel slamming, full impact, upon her knuckles.

131

When Rose tried to rise up to intervene, Sam wildly shoved her to the floor, enjoying the battle. Adrenaline flowing, he continued to hit Ruby with the paddle. The sound and the sight were too much for Rose, so she turned her face into a corner and covered her ears.

"You're so strong, aren't you Rose? When the going gets tough, what do you do? You turn your back on your little sister, and let her take a whoopin' for your big mouth!" Sam intended for his words to stab Rose with shame. As he raged, he continued to hit Ruby with that paddle, which was an extension of his own pent-up issues. "Look, Ruby, your sister loves you so much that she turns her back on you."

Whack.

Whack.

"Stop it! Please, stop!" Rose screamed. Although her ears were covered with her hands, she could still hear the paddle making contact with her sister, who was sobbing uncontrollably, now finding it difficult to catch a breath.

Each time Ruby screamed and each time Rose begged, it fed the dragon's lust for punishment. Finally, Ruby stopped screaming and crying. She just took it. All of it.

Miss Charity, still bound by the duct tape, watched in horror. She'd never encountered anything remotely like this before and didn't know what to make of it. Tears rolled down her face, and her heart called out for help. Immediately, her angel appeared in the closet with them. The little girl's eyes lit up when she saw him because she knew he would make everything all right. He touched Ruby's head, and she passed out cold, falling to the floor.

Rose, hearing her sister hit the floor, snapped her head around to see her now lifeless body. She shouted, "You killed her! Oh my God! You killed Ruby!"

Shocked, Sam rushed out, slamming the door shut behind him. Standing with his back against the door, he breathed fast and hard. His heart was pumping underneath his shirt, jarring his body. "Spare the rod, and spoil the child," he murmured, wondering if he'd actually killed the one he'd promised to protect. At that moment, he wasn't sure.

Rose crawled over to her sister and held her in her arms. "Ruby, please don't be dead," she cried. "Please, please don't be dead."

The angel tenderly removed all the duct tape from Miss Charity, setting her completely free. He patted her head and gave her a big smile. She quickly shimmied up into his lap. As Rose rocked Ruby in her arms, the angel rocked the little girl bearing the extra chromosome in his own arms. The house was quiet, and Rose wondered when Sam would come back and what he would do. Her breathing became audibly labored as panic rose, yet she didn't dare speak. She feared Sam would come back in and beat Ruby more if she breathed a word.

In the stillness of the moment, in the horror of it all, the angel began to sing. *"Amazing Grace, how sweet the sound, that saved a wretch like me..."* And as he sang, calm and peace fell into the closet, embracing them all. *"I once was lost, but now I'm found; was blind, but now I see."*

The angel kissed the top of Miss Charity's head before setting her back down upon the floor. He then scooted over to Rose and Ruby, who couldn't see him. Leaning down, he whispered into Rose's ear. "Rose, I am so sorry for all you've been through in your short life," he began, his voice breaking with each word. "This world is full of sin, and even innocent children are impacted by it every day. But you must never believe you don't have a choice to rise above it. Be strong and believe in the One who created you. Trust in the One who loves you with all His heart, and know that He will make beauty from your ashes."

Rose couldn't hear him, of course, but her spirit took in every word. Placing his hand upon Ruby's head, he commanded, "Wake up, Ruby!"

And she did.

Chapter 15

GiGi's reunion with her number-one grandson was not going as well as she'd hoped. Viv, after getting directions from Mary, pulled into the parking lot and quickly ran in to offer moral support. Finding the apartment door unlocked, she let herself in and found GiGi and Wills taking separate sides of an emotional war of words.

"Wills, it ain't normal for you to not speak to your GiGi and Poppy anymore. And what about your momma, Tate, and Miss Charity? Don't you think they need you?" She was trying to make a point by appealing to Wills's typical soft nature. "It's been weeks, Wills. What if I had keeled over and died? Wouldn't you have had regrets for how you've been out of touch with me?"

Neither Wills nor GiGi seemed to notice when Viv walked into the room, so she stood back by the door to watch and listen. Real tears were pouring from her mother's eyes, yet Wills seemed unmoved. When he didn't respond, GiGi made one last-ditch effort to get through to him. Her high-pitched squeal had not penetrated the stoned-face boyish countenance standing before her, only three feet away. She wanted so badly to take him in her arms and hug him, to ruffle his hair, to poke him in his ribs to get a giggle. But something was very different about him. There was a coldness in his eyes she hadn't seen before. Lowering her voice, and dropping all signs of attitude, she continued.

"Wills, darling, when we forced you to leave home to get out on your own, it was because we hoped it would be a wake-up call for you, an intervention of sorts. Your partying had gotten out of hand, and you know we are teetotalers in our family. I don't even drink a root beer because it has the word 'beer' in it."

She watched him closely, looking for even a slight glimmer of the boy she'd always adored. All he would give in return was a blank stare. No emotion. "Wills, we all need family. Don't you miss us?" she asked.

Meeting her tone, he answered flatly, "I have all the family I need."

GiGi, in typical fashion, couldn't hide the fact that his statement took her by surprise. "What family, Wills? Are you talking about your friends…like the girl I met today who is covered in tattoos, smoking her cigarettes and talking smack with an old lady?"

Wills laughed, ran his fingers through his hair, and raised his voice again. "No, that's not who I'm talking about. But you know, I'm sick of you bashing my friends and my lifestyle…it's probably time for you to turn around and click your high heels on out of here."

Viv, put off by the smart-aleck inflection in his voice, marched forward, stood beside her mom, and placed her arm around her waist. "Don't speak to your grandmother like that, young man. Whether you believe she is right or wrong about you, she deserves your respect at all times. So why don't you pipe down your tone about ten or twenty notches."

GiGi appreciated Viv's support but honestly didn't want her to interrupt what she considered to be *her flow*. Wills had never been one of Viv's fans, and GiGi worried she might do more harm than good. "It's all right, Viv, your momma can take his back talk. I just want to get back to this family business." Turning to Wills, she asked a direct question. "Tell me who your wonderful new family is, just so I'll know."

Wills was hoping she would ask. His grandparents and his mother had kicked him out of their lives, and Tate... well, she had gone right along with it without putting up a fight. He was done with them. The betrayal was too much. Sure, he had disobeyed some rules and at times had been disrespectful, but he was their blood. When is it ever right for parents to turn their back on a child? To put their child out on the street?

Wills narrowed his eyes and smiled. "My family is my dad and my grandparents…my *other* grandparents."

GiGi felt the punch in the gut as reality sunk in. Aggie had waltzed into town and was stealing Wills right out from under her nose.

Chapter 16

When Mary informed Viv that Miss Charity had been left with Sam, Viv took off like a rocket toward home. Mary, more concerned about Wills than ever, didn't notice her sister's haste. She pulled out behind Viv and followed her down I-75 toward home. The entire drive, GiGi preached. If she had ever hated Aggie Montgomery with all her heart, she now loathed her in the deepest possible way. And Philip? Even Mary couldn't believe he had undermined them. Mary had fully explained their reasoning for going nuclear on Wills. By forcing him to move out of the house, by placing him in a situation where he would be responsible for his own choices and actions, their plan was to shock him into repentance and to nudge him toward submitting to authority.

Hadn't Philip supported the decision? He'd told Mary he understood the thinking behind the decision and that he hoped it would make Wills mature. Mary's mind was reeling as she fought to recall the details of their conversation, but all her mind could hear was her mother's incessant babbling about Aggie. "This is all about me, Mary, make no mistake about it! I was always prettier and smarter than that old bag, so she is knifing me in the back by swiping Wills."

"Mother, please, we have to be careful what we say about Aggie," Mary urged, sincerely hoping to redirect the conversation. "Tate is in the car, and the woman, however much you might dislike her, is her grandmother, too."

GiGi wasn't ready to listen to any defense of her enemy, no matter how sensible Mary might try to be. She fired back, "Dislike her? If she were thirsting for water on the side of a road, I wouldn't as much as spit at her. Did you even hear what I said, Mary? The woman has stolen Wills from us!"

How many times had Mary spoken to Philip since the day she'd told Wills to leave? They spoke at least two times a day, sometimes more. And he'd never once mentioned he was having conversations with Wills. He'd never told her he was seeing Wills and offering support to him.

"Mary," GiGi continued, "do you understand what this means?"

She did. Unless the entire family stuck together on the whole tough love thing with Wills, their plan to bring him to repentance would never work. His problem was entitlement—at least that's what she and her parents had decided. Spoiled rotten by his family since birth, he'd never wanted for anything. Even teachers, coaches, and friends, smitten by his handsome appearance and his good manners, had always been willing to give Wills a break.

No, life hadn't been perfect for Wills. He'd had his challenges and a few hard knocks just like everyone else. But, for the most part, the path had been paved with glorious acceptance for the boy wonder. This time was

144

different because true accountability had been doled out, and he hadn't known how to deal with not getting his way. So he'd turned to his father and his *new* grandparents.

"I know exactly what this means, Mom," Mary answered, feeling worn-out by life in general. She had lost Philip to Bonnie, had lost her faith in Jesus to a cult, and was now losing Wills, too. "It means we've lost him. We needed to be a united front to bring some intervention into his life. The alcohol, late-night partying, speeding tickets, and reckless behavior will lead him into danger. I see that and you see that, but he doesn't. All he sees is that we abandoned him."

As the profound picture took form within her mind, GiGi felt a heaviness in her heart. Their family had been through so much. "We warned Wills over and over again, Mary. The partying was getting out of hand—what else could we do?" she asked, already knowing the answer. They could've ignored it and then, if he were to be caught up in an accident, feel the agonizing guilt over not doing more to stop him. Or they could have done what they did…rise up and hold him accountable.

"We did the right thing," said Tate, the first words she'd spoken since leaving the apartment. "I couldn't live if I knew he'd died from drinking too much and we just let him."

Tate. Mary hadn't thought of her or Miss Charity and how this was affecting them. Wills had not only been their big brother, he'd been their protector, the one who wore a cape around the house claiming to be their superhero. Teasing them relentlessly, Wills was the one who made them both laugh the loudest. A true competitor, he'd taught Tate to play basketball…and a kid at heart, he'd watched hundreds of Sesame Street episodes with Miss Charity. Until alcohol had entered his life, by all counts Wills had been the best big brother ever.

"Tater Bug, this is just as big a loss, if not bigger, for you and our Little Miss, and I am so sorry." Mary's words fell like dirty rain in the car, coating them all in deep, soot-like sorrow. How do a young teenager and a nonverbal child who has Down syndrome process such things? It wasn't fair. Sin is never fair.

Chapter 17

Philip wasn't surprised when Wills called him to tell him about how GiGi had paid him an unwelcome visit. His conniving eldest child had called Pip and Aggie first, and they'd already contacted Philip to encourage him to support his son. The truth of the matter was that he actually wanted very much to side with Mary and her parents on this latest debacle with Wills, but given how his life had been going, with the penis photo being passed around town and all, he needed every bit of support he could muster. Wills happened to be on the short list of the few who weren't avoiding him as if he were the plague.

Thankfully, Philip's lessor had agreed not to breach his contract, which allowed him some financial breathing room. Still saving every penny that was needed for necessities, he planned to purchase the Ocoee Street home again and to ask Mary to marry him all over again.

It would take a lot of work on his part to gain her trust back, but he was more than willing to put in the work required.

The nights had been excruciatingly lonely for Philip, so when Bonnie called to invite him to accompany her for dinner, he eagerly accepted. Their love affair was old news, and because she was involved in a sordid love affair with her new boss, he saw no harm in it.

They met at Roma, her favorite spot in town, and Philip was surprised to see she had reserved the entire space just for them. Bonnie, looking as sexy as ever, wore a black strapless minidress with spiked red heels. What was it about red heels that made Philip lust? She remembered. Bonnie clearly remembered.

"What's the occasion?" Philip asked, slurring his words because his mouth was now as dry as cotton.

Bonnie's hair was swept up high into a messy bun, and her makeup had strategically been applied to accentuate

149

her big sparkling eyes. Instead of answering him, she stood tall and allowed him to take her in. Confidence exuded from the blonde. It always did.

Philip, unable to deal with the silence, asked again, "Bonnie, what's the occasion?"

This time she answered. "Let's just say, I thought we might celebrate our friendship tonight."

The woman lacked nothing; even her counterfeit intent was spot on. She knew if Philip detected a hint of her actual plan, he would walk out…for Mary's sake, but not for his own sake. So she played the game he needed to play, the game she knew he wanted to play.

Bonnie had planned everything out to perfection. Philip's favorite music, which basically amounted to a blend of Hall and Oates, the Commodores, the Eagles, and Journey, serenaded them through the speakers as they waited for their food to be freshly prepared.

"Wanna dance?" Bonnie asked, reaching out her hand to Philip.

Shaking his head, he declined, knowing full well that dancing would put him way too close to Bonnie's body.

She wasn't ready or willing to take no for an answer, though, so she teased him. "But I believe that's the Eagles I hear...isn't that your favorite group of all time? C'mon, let's dance for the Eagles."

"Dancing would seem sort of awkward, wouldn't it?" he asked, now on the fence.

Grabbing Philip by the arm, she cleverly added, "Well, we are waiting for our food, and we have this whole place to ourselves, so I say...let's dance, handsome."

He did love the Eagles and hadn't danced in such a long time. How long had it been since anyone had paid much attention to him, other than to mock him for the now famous "penis photo"? Yet here was the gorgeous

Bonnie Cutless, dressed up like a supermodel, and she had gone to a lot of trouble to prepare a nice evening just for him. Yes, he should dance with her. Philip, of course, had no idea that Bonnie had already informed the staff to hold dinner until the two were seated. She hoped to be in his arms for a very long time.

Chapter 18

When they pulled into Viv's driveway, Mary was the one who went in to retrieve Miss Charity. Her heart was already reeling from the episode with Wills, so seeing a bright red mark on her daughter's face nearly wrecked her. Viv was already in the house wearing a blank stare, dreading the moment her sister laid her eyes on the Little Miss.

Sam, ever the sham artist, was armed with a story and quickly explained that Rose had struck Mary's little girl. He explained how the girls were playing so nicely together, how he had fallen asleep watching television, and how the next thing he remembered was being awakened by Miss Charity's shrill cry. When he found her, Rose was standing over her.

"It was obvious to me," he explained, "that Rose saw that she could take advantage of Miss Charity because I was sleeping." He actually worked up a few tears. "I feel just awful about this, Mary, I really do."

Mary had swept her little angel up into her arms and holding her close, stared down both Rose and Ruby, the delinquents. "How could you do this, Rose? What is wrong with you?"

Rose just stared at her, unmoved. She'd been blamed for so much during her short lifetime that she'd grown accustomed to it. Taking the rap and the punishment that went along with it usually worked better for her than telling the truth. So she stood and said nothing. Ruby, crying, stood by her side, also silent.

"Do you not even feel sorry for what you've done?" Mary asked, feeling angry.

Still the girls said nothing, and Rose stood resolute, not showing even a slight hint of emotion.

"Viv?" Mary turned toward her sister, seeking some sort of explanation.

Viv, not knowing what to say and feeling especially guilty since she'd bagged her responsibilities to be with Michael, simply shrugged.

GiGi, on the other hand, had plenty to say. "Sam, you are a colossal idiot. You knew full well these foster children are rough, but you still fell asleep on your job and let Rose wallop a little munchkin who not only can't fight back but can't tell us what happened. I have a good mind to go out in the yard, find a hickory stick, and beat you half to death with it. This isn't Rose or Ruby's fault at all. They are foster children. Do you hear me? Foster children. Lord, they probably beat the crap out of other kids for looking at 'em funny. You know better than this!"

She wasn't finished. "And Viv," she continued, ranting through a face that had already turned three shades of red, "why aren't you teaching these girls? They seem smart to me and can understand that Miss Charity has special needs. You have chosen to be their foster momma, so start being a momma."

Sam, not knowing whether Rose or Ruby might, in a moment of weakness, tell the truth, butted in. "Listen, I took care of everything. I gave Rose a good spanking. She won't do this again, I assure you of that."

Mary handed Miss Charity off to GiGi and knelt down before Rose and Ruby. "Is this true, Rose? Do you understand that Miss Charity has special needs? And have you learned your lesson?"

Rose nodded her head to indicate that she had learned her lesson, but fury burned inside her heart when she considered all Sam had done to Miss Charity and to Ruby. What burned her up even more was that she had to take all of the blame for someone else's actions. Sam had explained his course of action to the girls before the rest of the family returned and in the process informed Rose that he would "lay into Ruby with a whoopin' like she's never had" if she even thought about telling the truth. Even though she was a young girl, in her heart she hated Sam. He was smarter than most of the foster parents she'd dealt with and recognized that Rose's one weakness was her younger sister. He used it against her at every turn.

Rose was contemplating all these things when she was snapped back into reality by Mary's bony arms. The woman had taken both Rose and Ruby into her arms and embraced them tightly. Rose was taken by surprise. Mary, crying out loud, squeezed them as she sobbed.

"I'm sorry I got mad at you girls," she cried. "I should've been more considerate than to bring Miss Charity over here on your turf when this is your brand-new home and family. I can see why you'd feel threatened. This is all my fault, girls."

Ruby couldn't stand it. She threw her arms around Mary's neck and bawled like a baby. She'd never seen any adult take the blame for anything, and here Mary was taking the blame for something Sam had done. Overcome with sudden love for Mary, she laid her face in the kind woman's neck and let her tears flow. Rose, however, remained frozen, seemingly unmoved. She would never trust anyone except herself.

Chapter 19

"So your boss is your lover? Don't you feel guilty about that since it was his wife who helped you at the mental health facility?" Philip asked as he cut into a large portion of chicken parmesan. Then he added, "She's the reason you have this job, right?"

Bonnie giggled. "Why do you care about who I'm sleeping with?"

Philip realized he'd crossed over into a territory that was more personal than he'd intended. "Oh, I apologize... I've overstepped," he said, hoping not to give away his real interest in Bonnie's personal life. He couldn't put his finger on why he was suddenly interested, but the truth was, the man wanted to know everything about her.

Bonnie, in response, wanted very much to keep her love interest hanging on. "Oh, you haven't overstepped...we were naked together once upon a time, remember?" She let the words hang for a moment, hoping he would remember. She was certain his face turned a bit red, which meant he was engaged, so she gushed on. "My boss lives separate from his wife and has for years. They both date other people, sort of like me and Carter do. Nowadays, it's cheaper to stay married than to divorce, you know?"

Philip listened, taking in Bonnie's red lips and perfectly straight teeth as she spoke. The woman was gorgeous. She explained how the affair had ended, how it had been more recreational than anything else, and how Philip had been the only man she'd had real feelings for in a long time.

"But you will always love Mary…because you are loyal…and I admire that about you." She was speaking so fast that Philip was barely keeping up. He'd been sitting quietly, saying nothing, until it dawned on him that Bonnie had just admitted to caring about him. At least…she had admitted to caring about him at one time. "Not many people are loyal anymore, you know?" she continued without missing a beat, still nervously rattling on.

"Bonnie," Philip whispered, clearing his throat, trying to find a sound that would come out. "Bonnie," he tried again, this time making some progress, but his voice still broke. "Did you just say that you used to have feelings for me?"

Here was the moment Bonnie had been waiting for. The whole evening had been planned for this. She knew if she played her cards right, if she were patient, unassuming, and sexy as hell, she could make another play for the man she wanted more than the air she breathed. Mary's husband. The man who had treated her son, Crew, like he was his own son. "Yes, Philip, I had very real feelings for you. Other men have been recreational, but not you. Far from it." She looked into his eyes as she spoke, so he would know she meant every word.

Philip couldn't believe it, but he was actually thinking he might sleep with Bonnie again. How long had it been since he'd been intimate with a woman? Mary had been the only lover in his life aside from his brief affair with Bonnie. He couldn't count the number of months or days or hours, but his body was telling him it had been too long.

His cell phone buzzed. It was Mary. Looking across the table at Bonnie, he felt a sudden pang of regret. He'd cheated on his wife, the mother of his children, with this woman. And here he was. With her. Again.

He answered the call. The phone had been lying on the table, face up. Bonnie knew who was on the other end.

"Chief," Mary said, her voice tense and angry, "you're not going to believe this."

Without asking whether it was a good time to talk, Mary ran down her day in sequential order, beginning with how upset she'd been over Wills, how abandoned she'd felt by her own son. She then explained how she'd left Miss Charity with Sam, believing Viv would be there to help care for her…and how Viv had decided to join her and GiGi on the hunt for Wills in Chattanooga. Philip listened without interjecting, feeling horribly guilty for the part he'd played in further separating Mary and Wills. He again took in the beauty of Bonnie, who sat patiently only a couple of feet away. Reaching across the table, she touched his hand gently, rubbing her fingers up and down his. In response, his mind wondered about the man he'd become.

"Chief? Are you hearing what I'm saying?" Mary asked, in full frantic mode.

He had zoned out for a moment. "Yes, you were talking about how rejected you feel by Wills, and I am so sorry about all of this, Mary." Bonnie's hand was still touching his, making his complete engagement with Mary difficult.

The cell phone was on speaker in the car, and GiGi, upon noting that Philip was only half paying attention to his conversation with Mary, grabbed the phone. "Listen up you numskull, this is GiGi on the phone now. I *will* get your attention one way or another, so you'd be better off *choosing to hear* what Mary is trying to tell you." The woman had a way with words. Philip yanked his hand away from Bonnie and stood up ready to listen. "I'm going to put my daughter back on the phone now, so you better clean out your oversized ears and listen up!" she exclaimed, speaking with as thick a Southern drawl as Hoke Coburn in *Driving Miss Daisy.*

"Here, Mare Bear," she purred like a harmless kitten, coming down off her high horse in time to hand the phone back to Mary. "He's ready to listen to you now."

Mary again explained the happenings at Sam and Viv's, about how she'd found Miss Charity with a distinct red handprint on her face. She told him about how Sam had placed the blame on Rose and how the little girl hadn't denied the accusation. "But, Chief, I'm telling you, that handprint seems much bigger than Rose's hand. I think Sam may have done it."

Chapter 20

Wills met his grandparents, Pip and Aggie, at the Rebel for lunch. It was the restaurant where his dad often met Preacher Walker, but he had already checked with his dad and knew they wouldn't be there. Without anyone else in the family knowing, Wills had been meeting his grandparents weekly. Not only did they offer him moral support, but they also offered him financial support. A meeting with Pip and Aggie meant cash for Wills. As he saw it, the two didn't quite know what to do with themselves since retirement had set in and given them so much extra time, so he might as well be their hobby. It suited them all, him especially.

After being treated to a burger, tater tots, chili, and all the soda he could drink, Wills left with a hundred-dollar bill in his pocket. It would buy him enough marijuana to get through the party he and his friends had planned for the following weekend. Wills's supplier was a pre-pharmacy student at UTC and one of the guys he was currently rooming with. Everyone in his family had had a hissy fit when they learned he was drinking alcohol, but if word ever got back to them about his latest drug of choice, they would likely lock him up and throw away the key.

The problem with Wills's family, from his perspective, was that they were too old school. His grandparents and parents had been raised in the Southern Baptist Church tradition…attending weekly revivals, vacation Bible school, and Wednesday night mission studies. They were outdated, and there was no possibility of them ever catching up. In response, Wills had done all he knew to do. It was either fight with them over something he never intended to change or move on. So he was now living a separate life. At times he felt sorry that he no longer spoke to his mother on a daily basis, because for most of his life they'd been extremely close. Most of the time, though, she never entered his mind. Wills was an adult now, and it was time to let go of the past.

Preacher Walker, at GiGi and Poppy's urging, had tried to remain in touch with Wills, to no avail. Wills never answered his calls or texts, so eventually he gave up. He'd been a pastor for so many years that he'd seen this type of spiritual rebellion all too often. Wills had been one of his favorite young men, one he held in high regard with much hope, so it stung to see the boy fall away from his faith. The last time they'd spoken, Wills had explained that he still bought into God, believing Him to be the Creator, and that he also believed in heaven. But he'd decided that God wasn't as big and involved in his life as he once believed Him to be.

He'd explained to the older man: "There's no way God can possibly be involved in every aspect of everyone's life at the same time. That's so small-minded."

Wills's newfangled religion included comparing himself to others. By his own estimation, he was doing better than at least half the world, so he was good. And when things became complicated, he knew the sinner's prayer by heart: "Oh, God's never-ending grace. Confess and be forgiven."

After purchasing his stash, Wills decided to make a Walmart run to grab the grub he'd need to provide for the party. The weed had only cost him eighty bucks, so he had twenty left over to purchase some chips and dip. What he didn't know was that his other roommate, also a pre-pharmacy student, had turned both Wills and his supplier in to the school authorities. Apparently, the idea of a fellow pre-pharmacy student dealing in drugs had not set well with him. The timing couldn't have provided a more perfect storm, because in an effort to find one of the major suppliers, the Tennessee Bureau of Investigation (TBI) had eagerly gotten involved and had planned a sting operation around Wills. On the way to Walmart, he was busted.

When the authorities pulled him over, they found the marijuana, still in the plastic ziplock bag, hidden beneath his seat. Wills tried his best to talk his way out of it. The boy who had once reveled in his love for God, lied, cried, and begged, but it did no good. He was young and still new to the whole twisted drug universe. What he couldn't understand was how his arrest was much bigger than his small stash in the ziplock bag. The fact that he'd only been smoking for a few weeks didn't matter. The fact that he only smoked on the weekends at parties didn't matter either. The TBI was after a big fish, and Wills was the little bait fish who was going to lead them to him.

Chapter 21

The evening had been quiet and nondescript for the most part. The scent of microwave popcorn still hung in the air, and Preacher Walker, donning his blue-and-white striped pajamas, was busy reading through his sermon notes. As for Jeannie, she was already in bed, sound asleep, tucked in for the night. A tap at the door was unexpected but not completely out of the ordinary. The man had been a pastor for more years than he'd like to count and had grown used to being summoned at all hours of the day and night.

GiGi was frantic, which wasn't too unusual. Viv, at her side, was trying to calm her down when he opened the door, but it clearly wasn't working.

"I am so sorry to surprise you like this," GiGi rattled off rather loudly as she pushed her way into his living room, "but I couldn't talk to you on the phone about something this sensitive since our cell phones are probably being tapped in to or bugged. God! Who knew it would come to this!"

Preacher Walker, trying to process what the woman was saying, followed close behind both her and Viv. GiGi, plopping down on their long navy sofa, folded her arms and continued. "Listen, you better go get Jeannie and put something on to cover up your jams, because we're gonna be here awhile."

Without saying a word, the older gentleman turned and went to wake Jeannie.

Several minutes passed before the two, wrapped in blankets, returned to the living room. Jeannie, giving GiGi a sideways look, dared her to comment. "I know my hair's a mess and I'm not wearing a stitch of makeup, but I don't need you hazing me all night. Right now, just say whatever you're thinking and let's get it over with."

Without missing a beat, GiGi snickered. "You look just awful. Do you think you could go run a comb through your hair and add a touch of blush to your cheekbones?"

"No," Jeannie responded flatly. "Are we done?"

GiGi shook her head. "Not quite. Do you have a big grocery sack you could put over your head? If you'll fetch me some scissors, I can cut out some eyeholes for you, and it won't take but just a second."

"No," Jeannie answered, smiling this time. "Can we please be done?"

GiGi grinned. "I'm just teasing you, but you have given me a much-needed laugh because, God help you, honey, you do look a sight."

The both laughed. They'd been friends for such a long time that laughter came easy for them.

"All right, you squawkin' birds," the pastor interrupted. "Let's get to talking about what's so important that it's dragged us all up this time of the night." He made it known that he was not willing to listen to the women hemming and hawing all night. It was time to get down to the matter at hand, whatever that was.

"This time of the night?" GiGi shot back, mocking Preacher Walker. "It's barely seven, and you need to know that it ain't normal to go to bed before the chickens do."

Ignoring the jab from GiGi, Preacher Walker and Jeannie listened as she continued to unload. From Wills leaving home and having nothing to do with them to finding out that Aggie and Pip had been, without their knowing it, financially supporting his drug habit. There was no humor in her voice when she spoke, especially when she brought up the fact that Wills had been arrested for drug possession.

Preacher Walker was shocked, unaware that things with Wills had spiraled so out of control. He'd met with Philip often, but the man had never mentioned how bad things

174

were. GiGi was quick to explain how Philip was in cahoots with his parents in supporting Wills, and even though they were unaware he was into drugs, they still should've done a much better job communicating with the rest of the family.

"I mean, this is Wills we're talking about," GiGi explained. "As you know, Preacher, he was a fine upstanding Christian until Philip dragged the whole gosh-darned family into that cult fiasco. The boy is confused, so that's why he's turned to the weed."

Preacher Walker chuckled. "I can assure you, Wills is not confused about weed."

GiGi didn't appreciate the tone and was quick to let him know. "What then, pray tell, do you think the problem is? You've been his pastor since the time he was born, so exactly what did all your teaching do for him?"

Preacher Walker, quite used to being dressed down by his parishioners whenever feathers were ruffled, answered her question with a question. "Is that why you're here? Do you want Jeannie and me to help you try to find a solution for Wills?"

"No!" she snapped back. "I've got bigger fish to fry. I'm here about Mary."

Chapter 22

How many hours had passed since she died? Mary didn't know for certain. The one thing she definitely knew, though, was that she was dead. Definitely dead. It was the only thing that made sense. The news about Wills's arrest had been the catalyst that had brought her face-to-face with the tragic but freeing truth.

God loved Mary. She knew He did. From a young age, she'd served Him with a whole heart. Sure, she'd wrestled with Him on a few occasions, but all in all, she'd dedicated her life to her faith. Scripture, in its purest sense, had portrayed her heavenly Father as a daddy who would never give bad gifts to His children. As much as she loved her own children, her Creator loved her immeasurably more. The God she had known her entire life would never allow her to go through such heartache and turmoil. The only solution? She was dead.

Miss Charity's heart issue was so much to bear. Mary's youngest had been born with Down syndrome and had remained nonverbal, but the challenges that came with those factors paled in comparison to the uncertainty of the inoperable aneurysm that had been caught trespassing in her heart. It was an unwelcome intruder that no doctor could extract. As Mary thought about this from her new perspective, she knew *her* God would never allow her to go through such a thing. This had all been a bad dream. A death dream.

Then there was the matter of Wills. How could she have ever believed her near-perfect son would turn to alcohol, drugs, partying, and sexual promiscuity? She was almost embarrassed that she'd allowed herself to buy into such a nightmare. This was one of God's tests. Maybe the Catholics had it right all along. Was she in purgatory? Being faced with her worst fears as a sort of test? Yes, that had to be it. Wills, her firstborn, the one she loved the most because she'd loved him the longest—and the one out of everyone in her family who understood her most—would never *leave* her. Absolutely not. He had the kindest heart of anyone she'd ever known. It wasn't in his DNA to forsake his family, especially not her.

Last, but not least, there was Philip. He'd been her one and only love…always trustworthy, honest, and true. The first clue she was in some sort of death dream should've been when he had the affair with Bonnie Cutless. Philip loved his family too much to fool around. How could she ever have believed such a thing? Yes, this was definitely a test of some sort.

Mary lay on her bed, finally at peace, contemplating her new truth. She didn't need pills, alcohol, counseling, or therapy. What she'd needed all along was truth. It had been staring her in the face, luring her to see, but she'd been so caught up in the contrived hurt to allow herself to consider that she was dead. When her mind had first contemplated a death dream, it had sounded ludicrous, but now it made all the sense in the world.

She and Philip were much too strong in their faith to ever fall prey to a cult. She laughed as she envisioned herself wearing those long Amish skirts with the little doily on her head. "I was a kook!" she said out loud to herself. "I definitely failed that test."

She continued to recount how Philip had invested all their money into the cult's vision…only to lose it all. And how, as a result, they'd lost their beloved home. Looking around her bedroom, in the home she'd previously thought to have been transferred to her parents, she realized she wasn't in the house at all. She was either six feet under, buried in the ground, or she was mere ashes in a jar. The thought gave her a few uneasy butterflies in her stomach, but Mary had resolve. She'd been tricked by the enemy; that was the only explanation. In this state of purgatory, God obviously allowed the enemy to continue his tricks. Even in death, up until Christ's return, she imagined she'd be tested. From now on, however, Mary would be prepared. The enemy wouldn't steal heaven away from her. She just had to remind herself that what she perceived to be real wasn't real at all.

After much contemplation, Mary finally nailed down the date of her death to Miss Charity's birth. Her blood pressure had bottomed out many times during childbirth, and she recalled how concerned the medical team had been. At some point during the birthing process, she must have died. As she thought back upon the experience, she remembered how different she'd felt after her youngest daughter's birth, but at the time she had attributed it to the fear that comes with being a mom to a special needs child. Now she realized she had died that day, which meant in reality, Philip was raising Miss Charity as a single father. A widower. It also meant that Wills and Tate were right by his side. Her family, outside her horrible death dream, was very much intact. Perfectly intact and magnificently strong.

Deciding she'd continue to go through the motions of her death dream every day, Mary climbed out of bed to clean the house. She patted the walls, stomped the floors, and hugged both Tate and Miss Charity as tight as she could. It all felt so gloriously real. Seeing a bruise on the arm of Miss Charity, her thoughts went to Sam Smith. To her mother and to Philip, she'd accused Sam of hitting her daughter. It now seemed absurd.

"It was another test," she said, sweeping the kitchen floor, "and I failed because of my lack of faith."

Tate, watching TV in the great room, responded, "Did you say something to me, Mom?"

The death dream was remarkable. No detail was missed. It was just like real life. Death dreaming resembled *living* in every way. "I was just saying that I love you, honey-bunch," she answered happily, just playing along with the dream.

"Oh, I love you too, Momma," Tate said, turning to grin at Mary.

Mary's heart felt the warmth that only comes from child to mother. She was glad she was in this death dream, because to be dead, and for death to be nothingness, would mean that she'd be missing her children so much. This wasn't an ideal scenario, but she appreciated that it kept her in contact with her family.

Continuing to sweep, Mary again thought of Sam. This man, in her death dream, had married her sister and had made her sister happy. If he were real, he was a good man. Viv was too smart to ever marry an abusive man who would harm her—or worse, harm a child. The truth was that Miss Charity had never been hit at all, which meant that she must have some unresolved issue with Viv that needed to be fixed before she could move on through that part of the test.

"Am I jealous of Viv?" she asked herself. She didn't feel jealous. But if Mary's goal was to pass on to the next level of this state of death, to awaken from this stage of her death dream, she had to figure out how to work through each test.

Tate, who was comfortably sprawled out on the sofa, jerked around to look at Mary. "Mom, are you talking to yourself?"

Laying the broom against the wall, Mary jogged over to the sofa and plopped down right beside Tate. "I was just thinking about Aunt Viv. Do you think she and I have a good relationship?"

"I guess so," Tate answered, shrugging her shoulders.

"Would you say I'm jealous of her?" Mary asked, hoping not to freak her daughter out. Although she believed wholeheartedly that she was in a death dream, there was still a slight chance that this was actually reality. And just in case, she didn't want to wreck what was left of her daughter's foundation.

Tate furrowed her brow. "You're being weird today."

"Well, then, answer your weirdo mom's question." Mary tickled her daughter's toes as she spoke.

"If you'll stop tickling me, I'll answer you," Tate howled.

Mary did.

"I think Aunt Viv is probably jealous of you because you're so beautiful."

Mary, sincerely flattered, hugged her daughter tight. Tate had a good heart, and it was impossible for her to believe anyone on earth could ever be greater than her momma. "You are the kindest person I've ever known, Tater Bug, did you know that?" A tear escaped Mary's eye as she considered the fact that this was only a death dream. She felt a pang of regret, as she wished she'd spoken those words to Tate when she was still a part of the living. "I was so blessed when God chose me to be your mom."

Tate, seeing her mother's tears, pulled Mary's head down to her shoulder and kissed her head. "Sit with me, OK, Momma? It's late, and you've been working around the house all day."

Mary settled in close to Tate, and as the TV blared out a recorded episode of *I Love Lucy*, Mary allowed her mind to wander. In Mary's death dream, Miss Charity was sleeping soundly in her bedroom. In reality, however, she wondered what she was doing. Was she healthy? Did she know she had a mother who loved her? And why would God make her a part of the death dream? As she mulled over all the possibilities, she decided her biggest test was faith. She held onto her children so tightly. Too tightly. In the death dream, she had to hand Miss Charity's heart issue over to God. She had to trust Him with all of Wills's rebellion. She had to trust Sam and to reunite with Philip. But most importantly, she had to learn to love with abandon. Mary decided her death dream could possibly turn into a fantastic dream come true if she'd act more like Jesus.

Her first step would be to contact Sam Smith and to allow him to babysit Miss Charity again.

Second, she'd deal with Wills. She'd tell him she accepted his drug habit, his promiscuity, and his rejection of her. She would return his rejection and his sin with so much love that he'd choke and drown in it.

Next, she'd win Philip's heart back and beg for his forgiveness. As for Bonnie, if she ever saw the woman again, she'd just treat her like a sister. "There was never an affair," she giggled, sincerely happy as she thought about it.

"Momma, why do you keep babbling?" Tate asked, still cuddled close to her side. "Just be quiet and watch TV with me."

Mary, being cute, took her fingers and pretended to lock her lips shut and then throw away the key. Tate seemed appeased and returned her mother's actions with a cute wink.

Mary's mind, though, continued to wander and to wonder. Finally, she decided she would not worry another second about Miss Charity's heart defect. All the sleepless nights were over, because Mary believed she was living in a death dream. She would choose to believe Miss Charity lived in perfect health. She even allowed herself to imagine her daughter speaking real words to Philip, to Tate, and to Wills.

To face these things with faith and love would surely bring Mary to a new level of immortality. If this death dream was a test, well…she would pass with flying colors. The woman was ready to let it all go and to give control of her death to God.

Chapter 23

The attorney was old. Lem Lawson had been in private practice for fifty years and had made a boatload of money taking on the medical field and local corporations for malpractice and negligence. A remnant of gray hair encircled the lower half of his head; he wore it like a crown. Wills sat across the table from him, unimpressed. Lem and his fifteen-hundred-dollar tailored suit were too slick. By Wills's estimation, any man over the age of sixty who bleached his teeth and spray tanned his body was *not* to be trusted. Sure, he was known for being the best defense attorney in the area, possibly in the state, but there was something about him that didn't sit right. Pip and Aggie were impressed with his winning statistics, but what caught their attention most was that he'd defended a few drunk driving cases where a fatality was involved and had managed to create enough doubt to get the drivers off on probation. Lem was known for drama, and the courtroom was his stage. He owned it (along with most of the judges in town).

"In the state of Tennessee, for first-time drug possession, you can definitely count on a misdemeanor charge but possibly a felony charge," Lem advised, showing no emotion. "It's up to the judge. With the Class A misdemeanor charge, you will face up to a year in jail and a twenty-five-thousand-dollar fine. Count on it." Looking over his silver rectangular spectacles, his brow wrinkled as he waited for their response. He'd laid out the bad news. He'd given them the facts. Now it was their turn to entreat him for his services.

Wills was hoping to be encouraged, but the attorney's words were anything but comforting. It was marijuana, not cocaine or heroin, and it was legal in some states already (used for medical purposes) and was less addictive than alcohol. Yet it was going to cost him his reputation. With a record, what would his future hold? "They want me to rat out my supplier, but he's not the one they're really after," Wills explained, deciding to put his cards on the table. "They want to use my supplier to get to one of the sources. As you know, ratting out a drug dealer could get me and my friend killed."

"Killed?" Aggie interjected. "I think that's a bit exaggerated. Surely to God no one would *kill* Wills over something like this, right?"

Lem didn't flinch. "It depends on this particular drug ring. There are some scary fellas who make a lot of cash in this industry, and they will not be happy if a punk college kid puts a kink in their routine." He took his glasses off, turned them around to peer into the glass, breathed on them, and then yanked his handkerchief from his pocket to clean them. A master of theatrics, those few moments of silence served his objective perfectly. "It sounds to me like Wills needs a good defense attorney." He smiled, put his glasses back on, and patted the desk. "That's why you're here, I'm guessing."

Chapter 24

As GiGi recounted every detail of the trials and tribulations being brought to bear on her family, Preacher Walker and Jeannie listened closely. The old pastor's thoughts turned toward Job from the Bible as he considered Mary. Job, after losing his material possessions, his family, and his health, was at a place where an honest evaluation of his heart could take place. It's so easy to believe in God and to trust God when life is easy. When the storms come, however, destroying everything, that's when we either sink or swim. That's the time when our faith strengthens or when it dies. The entire family was at a crossroads, but Mary, in particular, was caught in the eye of the destruction.

"If you study Job," the pastor interjected, "there were some who thought he was losing his mind. Remember how his friends questioned him?" He was clearly thinking out loud, but he wanted to hear the others' thoughts on the subject. "Maybe Mary isn't losing her mind at all. Perhaps she's just being tested."

GiGi, still reeling from all the varying emotions she'd been juggling, blurted out, "Death dream…what about that? Does it not say that Mary is losing her ever-loving mind, Preacher?" Rubbing her face with her hands, she shook her head in despair. Her family was falling apart.

Preacher Walker, seeing her grief and worry, responded with a gentle warmth. His voice, calm and reassuring, spoke directly to her heart. "GiGi, we've known each other a long time. And as you know, I love your family like my own. For whatever reason, the devil has asked permission from the Lord to test y'all. Trust me, Mary's death dream is part of this test. Wills's rebellion is part of the test. And Miss Charity…well, I believe she is the center of it all. That precious one is an angel. Mary will make it through this for her sake. I know it."

His eyes. There was something about them. They had this twinkle about them when he knew he was on to

193

some sort of hidden truth. GiGi had trusted in that twinkle more times than she could count, but this was bigger. This latest family drama seemed monumental to her.

"But I read it all in her journal. To her, none of us are real. Don't you see? She'll be making decisions based upon believing she's dead…living in a false reality." GiGi couldn't believe the words that were coming out of her mouth. When she and Viv started seeing a change in Mary's behavior, GiGi had done the unthinkable by sneaking into Mary's dresser drawer and reading her private journal. Now, of course, she was glad she'd been so nosy. "It sounds like she's gone cuckoo, and it's changed everything. Now when I'm around her, I literally walk around like…like…well, like a dead person. It's messing with my mind, too."

"It's messing with all our minds," Viv added.

GiGi put her arm around Viv's shoulder. "And to make matters worse, Mary believes Sam slapped Miss Charity the other day when he babysat her. I didn't say anything when she blamed him, because I know she's half nuts right now, but Lord Almighty, she can't go creating more trouble," GiGi huffed, making sure Viv felt her full support. "I may not always agree with Sam and his cult, but for heaven's sake, he isn't an abuser."

Viv's eyes immediately dropped to the floor as her face flushed. No one except Jeannie noticed. "Everything all right with you and Sam, honey?" Jeannie quickly asked, feeling a twinge of concern. Jeannie wasn't one for many words, but when she felt a tug, she went with it.

GiGi, not wanting to get off course, shot back, "Of course everything's OK with Viv and Sam. We came over here about getting the death dreams with Mary straightened out."

Viv nodded her head. "Mom is right," she said. "We've got to help Mary. She isn't well."

Out of the darkness of the night, a bright light shone in the front window. "Looks like we've got another visitor," Jeannie said, getting up and going toward the door. "I know I may go to bed with the chickens," she added, glaring in GiGi's direction, "but this is getting ridiculous." Peering out the window, she immediately recognized the vehicle. "Ladies, get ready, it looks like your death dreamer just pulled into the driveway."

Mary entered Preacher Walker and Jeannie's home with a smile, nearly floating on air. All her anxiety was gone now that she knew the truth about her death. Grinning from ear to ear, she explained how she'd left Tate at home with Poppy, and how she'd made arrangements for the women to spend a couple of nights in Nashville at the Opryland Hotel.

"I know it's a little late, but I've already packed your bags, GiGi and Viv! This will be a girls' getaway we should've done a long time ago."

GiGi turned to Viv and whispered, "She means before she died."

Viv gave her mother a knowing nod.

"Jeannie," Mary continued, "I want to invite you to come with us, too." Mary nearly sang the words. In her death dream, she would enjoy giving to others, she would worry less, and she would finally take the time to have fun.

GiGi answered for Jeannie. "Of course Jeannie will come with us, Mare Bare, and we will teach her how it is possible to enjoy life after seven o'clock." GiGi tried to appear lighthearted as she joked around about Jeannie, but unlike Mary, her voice was filled with trepidation. Her eyes, too, looked a bit wild. "Preacher Walker, you won't mind if Jeannie goes and gets a few things together, will you? It's just a couple of days, and it will do us all some good to get away together."

The pastor, taking GiGi's cue, urged Jeannie to go with them. "Go pack, old gal. I'll miss you, but I think you're needed more with these rascals right now than with me." He laughed. "Besides, maybe you can finally talk to some sense into all of 'em."

While Jeannie reluctantly packed, the preacher, Viv, GiGi, and Mary talked about Job from the Bible and all he'd gone through. "You know, Mary, you've been through a lot, too," the preacher added. "Maybe you're being tested just like Job was tested."

"Oh, I'm sure of it!" Mary responded with glee. "And I will pass this test with flying colors." Her face beamed. She appeared more at ease than she'd been in years. "I just want you all to know how much I love you. I haven't said it enough. I love you all to pieces."

GiGi, put off by Mary's good nature, made sure the pastor caught her glance. She silently mouthed, "See? She's gone crazy!" when Mary wasn't looking. The pastor shook his head with a stern look, letting her know

198

she needed to be careful about what she said and did behind Mary's back. It didn't stop GiGi. "She thinks she's dead," she mouthed again, holding her neck with her hands like she was choking herself. Again, the pastor shook his head. This time he mouthed the words: "Stop it!" And Mary noticed.

"Is something wrong?" she asked.

To change the subject, GiGi quickly jabbed, "I bet old Poppy's not too happy about having Tater and Miss Charity to care for over the next couple of days while we're partying at the Opryland Hotel in Nash-Vegas! But maybe he'll call on Philip, the penis man, for some help."

Jeannie walked in the room to catch the last part of what GiGi was saying. "I'm sorry, what did you say about Philip and his famous penis?" She laughed as she thought of how her longtime friend would never be able to get over how the whole town had seen her ex-son-in-law's private parts.

"I was just saying that Poppy will hopefully put his pride down and call Philip for help when he needs a break from Tate and Miss Charity," GiGi answered. "I know he lives with them, but that little bugger with the extra chromosome can be a handful."

Mary, waiting for the right moment to spring another piece of her news on them, jumped up from her seat. "Guess what?" she asked, barely able to contain herself and still smiling from ear to ear. "I've left Miss Charity with Sam overnight. He isn't working tomorrow, and he said he'd be happy to keep her all day, too. So Pops will only have both girls for one night. Aren't you proud of your hubs, Viv?"

Jeannie's eyes immediately darted over to Viv, who looked like the air had been depleted from her world. Viv's words, when she finally found them, were hushed and filled with fear. "You left Miss Charity with Sam? And the girls? Why would you do that?"

Mary didn't notice her sister's concern. Jeannie did.

"Oh, don't worry about Sam. He was happy to do it," Mary explained, quite proud of herself. "I just want Rose and Ruby to know that I trust them. And I want Sam to know I trust him, too. Today marks a new beginning for us all."

GiGi, this time, added her two cents. "Mary, the last time Miss Charity stayed with Sam and those girls, she came home with a bright-red hand mark across her face. You do recall that, right?"

"Of course I remember that…and I blamed Sam, which was horrible of me." Turning to her sister, Mary confessed, "Viv, I am so sorry. I know you would never stay with an abusive man; I don't know what I was thinking. Whatever happened with my little Miss Miss, I believe it was an accident. I don't know how I could've ever doubted you or Sam."

Viv was so dumbfounded, she couldn't speak. Her mind began playing out scenarios that frightened her, but what could she do? This was not the time or place to divulge the fact that Sam was a monster. Jeannie, noticing Viv's tension, stepped over and put her arm around her back. Something was very wrong.

Chapter 25

Miss Charity didn't know why her mother had dropped her off at Sam's house again. Being unable to speak had its definite disadvantages. If she could've spoken, she would have described all the fear she felt when they pulled into his driveway late at night. She'd overheard her mother speaking to Poppy and knew that she was going to be staying overnight with Sam, Rose, and Ruby. Her aunt Viv wouldn't be around.

"You'll have a great time," her mother had said. Oh, how she wished she could've told her mother about the horror she'd been through the last time she'd stayed with Sam. She remembered her mother seeing the handprint on her cheek and even recalled her mother telling both GiGi and her dad that she believed Sam was the culprit. Why the sudden change? Miss Charity was at a loss.

When they pulled into the driveway, the little one had tried to cry or scream or make some noise, but her mouth wouldn't cooperate. She couldn't manage a single sound. Then, when her mom began to undo the buckles of her car seat, she'd struggled and pushed her hands away, hoping she would get the hint. But Mary was in a hurry and didn't seem to notice. Pulling Miss Charity onto her hip, Mary had brought the lamb to the lion's den.

As soon as Mary was out of sight, Sam had replaced his warm smile with an angry face. Rose and Ruby weren't around. Miss Charity looked for them but didn't see them. It was just Sam and her. Alone. He'd called her a retard, tied her hands and feet with bands, and picked her up and thrown her onto the guest bed. Flat on her back, with her hands tied in front of her, she stared at the ceiling listening to Sam roar:

"You are a seed of Satan, and I will treat you as such. The Bible says God is perfect and that all He has created by His word is perfect. That means, retard, that when something or someone is imperfect, they have been tainted by Satan."

She didn't understand what he was saying, exactly, but she knew he was being hateful, and she knew he was angry. Not wanting to make Sam any madder at her, she lay very still and quiet, just looking at the ceiling.

"Don't worry, though, you aren't the only one who belongs to Satan," he continued, rattling on as if he were preaching a sermon. "Rose and Ruby are half-breeds, and that is unholy, too. You're a retard, and they are half-breeds. It is my calling to put each of you under the authority of the one true God. Scripture says to bind the enemy, and so you are bound, as are they. Your heart is weak and will explode one day soon. When it does, you will die and go to meet your maker in hell. And on that day, praise the Lord, I will rejoice at God's victory over sin."

Chapter 26

Viv, after assuring Jeannie that all was just fine with her, slipped into the guest bathroom to call Michael. He lived only a few miles from the house she shared with Sam, and she had a huge favor to ask him. Within minutes, he was in his car, ready and willing to secretly investigate her home. Viv had to make sure Sam was not abusing her niece, and Michael had agreed to her frantic plan.

Mary's car was packed with Viv, GiGi, Jeannie, and several overnight bags. They had just pulled onto the interstate when Michael called. She felt her phone buzz and slowly put it up to her ear, hoping no one would notice. Knowing her secret relationship with Michael had to remain a secret, she held the phone close to her ear as she peered out her window, not saying anything but listening closely.

"Babe, I'm here. I've parked down the street and am walking up to the house now. The lights are still on, so I should be able to get a look at what's going on inside."

She could hear his feet tromping over dried leaves and twigs. She and Sam lived on several acres, and most of it was wooded.

"If he is doing anything to harm Miss Charity or Rose or Ruby, I guess you'll want me to call the police?" he asked, trying to plan ahead. His heart was racing as adrenaline flooded his veins, but there was no turning back. Viv had confided in him about all the abuse, including how cruel he'd been to her, so he felt he had no choice but to step in and protect those who couldn't defend themselves. He'd fight for the girls' safety if necessary.

"No police," Viv whispered.

"Sweetheart, I know you don't want to be the star of a scandalous sex story around town, even though it has been a steamy scandal in my opinion, and even though you have been a super-hot costar"—he snickered, hoping his teasing would calm both their nerves a bit—"we do have to protect those girls if necessary."

As much as she hated the thought of it, Viv knew he was right. If Sam was abusing the girls, the authorities would have to be notified in order to protect them. The cost, however, would be tremendous. Her parents and sister would never forgive her for not telling them the truth about Sam, and if anything happened to Miss Charity, she would never forgive herself.

"I'm at the window, and it looks like Miss Charity is lying on the bed, and I think she's by herself. She looks safe to me, but I honestly can't tell whether he has her bound or tied down to the bed, thanks to the stupid sheers on the window…and I don't see Rose or Ruby in the room. I'll walk around the house and see if I hear anything that sounds suspicious, and then I'm out of here. Hold on while I make my way around; it will take me just take a couple of minutes."

Viv felt relieved. Perhaps she'd jumped to conclusions. Maybe Sam wouldn't harm Miss Charity. She held on the phone listening to Michael breathing as he walked. He had become more than her lover; he'd become her best friend, her confidant, and now, her hero. She'd called him, and without hesitation, he'd rushed to protect her family. Michael was the man of her dreams, and she would be with him as soon as they could figure out a way to safely set her free from Sam.

She was ready to hang up the phone, ready to refocus her attention on her trip to the Opryland Hotel in Nashville, ready to enjoy time away from Rose, Ruby, and Sam… until she heard Sam's voice. "Who the hell are you, and why are you prying around my house at this time of night?"

Viv went numb.

"I'm sorry. My car broke down, and I've been wandering around trying to find someone to help me." Michael's voice was shaky; he was panicking. "Could you put the gun down? I don't mean any harm; you can trust me."

"You expect me to buy that story? That you're a stranger out wandering the streets at night, trying to find a good Samaritan to help you out with your broken-down vehicle?" Sam asked. Viv thought she could hear Sam walking toward Michael, most likely still pointing his gun. "Tell me, Michael, did my wife send you over here to check up on me? Did she tell you I might abuse the kids? That I'm a crazy tyrant?"

His voice became louder and more clear, so Viv was certain he was continuing to take steps in Michael's direction as he taunted him with his words. It was all more than Michael and Viv could mentally process. He knew who Michael was?

"How is my wife in bed, Michael? Do you know what the Bible says about adulterers and fornicators? You probably don't since you're living like the devil, so I'll fill in the blanks for you. It says they deserve death…so, I reckon that means *you* deserve death."

Not only was Sam holding a gun, but he was pointing it at Michael. And he knew about their affair. The reality hit Viv like a ton of bricks. Sam was going to kill Michael.

Boom!

The sound of the gunshot rang in her ear. Mary nearly ran off the road when Viv screamed. No one in the car knew she was on the phone, so the guttural cry that came from her mouth was completely unexpected. All Viv could think was that Michael was dead. And she would be next.

Chapter 27

In an ordinary parsonage at the corner of hope and hopelessness knelt the old white-haired knee bender who was known as a praying man. Around him knelt four mighty angels who were unseen by him but whose very presence demonstrated the pastor's relationship with God. Each word he uttered was carefully captured in midair, the sound of his voice whirling around the room, being repeated by the angels, collecting the power of heaven and getting ready to go do its work.

The spoken word. It is what set the existence of space and time into motion, what put the sun and moon to work, what separated the sky from the sea, and what forced the first breath into man. Scripture teaches when great faith is mixed with word, it moves mountains, gives sight to the blind, and raises the dead. Our words, all of them, are never returned void. They accomplish either evil or good.

On this night, Preacher Walker, a modern-day shepherd who tenderly cared for those who'd been entrusted to him, was hoping his words would accomplish good. He'd seen miracles in his lifetime, things that could only be explained by the belief in something greater…by the belief in *Someone* holy, magnificent, and almighty. Just as often, however, he'd witnessed the reckless hand of the enemy and had seen the carnage left behind by one who is the opposite of God. With great expectation, not trusting the imperfection of his own words, the lowly servant recited the scripture he'd safely hidden within his heart.

It was part of the grand plan. The purpose. This journey was not about Mary, Viv, GiGi, Miss Charity, Wills, Philip, Bonnie, Preacher Walker, or Jeannie. It was about all of them, and it was just the beginning of what was to come.

Epilogue

Why do bad things happen to good people? It's a question as old as time itself. Instead of asking "Why me?" over and over again, we should probably consider asking "Why not me?" Sin is, in fact, no respecter of persons. It opens bolted doors, seeps into secured spaces, and transforms with chameleon-like savvy into innocent-looking, appealing weapons that can fool even the wisest of men. Created by God Himself, sin is a three-letter word that has infected every human life. Like air, it cannot be avoided.

So the conundrum remains: If sin brings destruction and death, what was God's motive behind its conception? Scripture clearly states He is a good Father who seeks to give good gifts to His children, but how is sin a good gift?

Clearly, there are two distinct sides that define earth: good and evil, God the Almighty and Lucifer the devil. When we erase the finite boundaries of space and time that dictate the world we live in and open our minds to what scripture reveals, we clearly see a battle for power that began *before* the creation of man. The devil, who was once a lead angel, was given what he wanted most: the opportunity to have his own kingdom. We are his opportunity. The enemy has been given full reign, with one caveat. It appears he must gain permission to tempt and torment those who belong to the Lord, which means each and every heartache, tragedy, sickness, disease, loss, and need has been sifted through the very hand of God. It's a difficult concept to accept, and it turns our feel-good Sunday morning church services upside down.

To be the all-knowing and all-present Sovereign God, though, He must have full authority. If not, He would not be God. There is therefore purpose in all things. Is He mighty to save us from destruction? Yes. Is He able to save us from tragedy? Yes. Does He always rescue us

215

from sin? No. Why? Because He is God, and His thoughts and ways are beyond ours. To belong to Him means to trust Him, no matter what. When life is the most difficult, in fact, the measure of our raw faith is on full display. How much glory must that bring to the King of Kings?

Oh, but friends, this is not the end. No, this is only the beginning of what is to come. One day, everything that is upside down will be turned over and made right. *That* is the God we serve. We *will* absolutely walk on streets made of gold where there will be no more poverty, discrimination, sickness, hurt, tears, or pain…where He will reign with full peace, and where we will all experience love perfectly. Wherever you are today, whatever you are going through, be reminded that this is only for a time and a season. Look toward the hills. He's coming for us!

"Though He slay me, yet will I trust in Him." (Job 13:15, King James Version)

www.ingramcontent.com/pod-product-compliance
Lightning Source LLC
Chambersburg PA
CBHW070821120626
46556CB00002B/607